HAMSTER IN THE HOLLY

"Oh, no!" Mandy gasped, staring at a gap in the front row of seats. It could only mean one thing.

"What?" James stared at her as if she'd gone crazy, his glasses glinting from a reflection of the overhead stage lights.

"Daniel's not in his seat!"

"So?" James turned around to face the stage. Any second now, the cymbals would clash, and Mandy would have to make her entrance.

"He's up to something," Mandy said. "I don't know what, but now I come to think of it, I didn't see him leave the biology lab with the rest of us. He could still be in there with Henry! And Honey and Marmalade!"

"Mandy, what are you saying?" James spread his hands helplessly.

"I don't know exactly!" she hissed. The cymbals clashed. She clenched her fists and got ready to enter.

"Stage fright," he muttered.

"No, James, I'm worried about the hamsters!"

Read all the Animal Ark books!

by Ben M. Baglio

$3.99 US Each!

ANIMAL ARK®

Hamster
in the Holly

Ben M. Baglio

Illustrations by Jenny Gregory

AN
APPLE
PAPERBACK

SCHOLASTIC INC.
New York Toronto London Auckland Sydney
Mexico City New Delhi Hong Kong Buenos Aires

ISBN 0-439-44893-X

Text copyright © 1998 by Working Partners Limited.
Created by Ben M. Baglio, London W12 7QY
Illustrations copyright © 1998 by Jenny Gregory.

14 13 12   5 6 7 8 9/0

Printed in the U.S.A.   40

With thanks to the children of
Worsthorne County Primary and
Ightenhill County Primary Schools, Burnley.

Special thanks to Jenny Oldfield.
Thanks also to C. J. Hall, B.Vet.Med., M.R.C.V.S.,
for reviewing the veterinary material
contained in this book.

One

"Twelve more days till Christmas!" Mandy Hope and her mother staggered into the kitchen at Animal Ark, loaded down with heavy shopping bags. Big snowflakes had settled lightly on Mandy's blond hair and they began to melt in the warmth.

"Watch out!" Adam Hope jumped up from his seat at the table. He cleared a space for the bags. "What did you and your mom buy, the whole store?"

Mandy put down the shopping bags. "Christmas favors, candles, cards, wrapping paper, tinsel, some new Christmas tree lights, some more silver ornaments, a new star for the top of the tree —"

1

"Whoa!" Her dad begged her to stop and went to help his wife with the rest of the shopping. "I was joking when I said the whole store!"

Mandy and her mom had driven into Walton after Saturday morning clinic hours. It was the next-to-last weekend before Christmas, and the small Yorkshire town where Mandy went to school had been crowded with people frantically buying presents.

"Never again!" Emily Hope said, taking off her thick jacket and shaking off the snow. "I don't want to see another Santa's workshop or hear 'Away in a Manger' ever again!"

"Hot chocolate!" Mandy's dad announced. "That's the remedy for tired shoppers."

Dr. Emily ran a hand through her long red hair, then looked at her watch. "Is there time? Afternoon office hours begin in fifteen minutes, and I want to pop into the residential unit to take a look at the Border collie with the broken ribs before that."

"Done it." Dr. Adam boiled some milk, then poured it into mugs and stirred in the chocolate powder. "And I've checked the duck with the cut foot, the cat with the eye infection, and the bull terrier with the gashed face."

"Oh, thanks!" Dr. Emily smiled and took a steaming mug. "Leave those bags for now, Mandy. Come and put your feet up for five minutes."

"I can't." Mandy pulled out the Christmas tree star. "James is coming to rehearse our parts."

James Hunter, Mandy's best friend, had arranged to come to Animal Ark to work with her on *The Little Mermaid*, Walton School's play.

"I thought wild horses wouldn't drag you and James onto a stage," Dr. Adam teased. "Isn't that what you've always said?"

"Please don't remind me!" Mandy took her mug to the window and saw James step out of his father's car, which had just pulled up.

"Don't you usually leave the prancing around, as you call it, to the likes of Susan Collins?"

"Da-ad!" Mandy pleaded. The thought of performing onstage in next week's show filled her with dread. "Mrs. Winterton *made* me."

"Count yourself lucky you don't have to wear a mermaid's tail." Dr. Emily smiled.

"Yes, but I have to *sing*!" Mandy wailed. She flounced out of the kitchen to open the door. "I have lots of complicated lines to speak. And worst of all, Mrs. Winterton says I have to learn how to cackle!"

"That's not a cackle, that's a croak," James pointed out in a bored voice. "Witches have this special laugh that's kind of thin and wicked. Try again."

Mandy sagged and sighed. Then she took a deep breath. *"Ha-ha! Aha-ha!"*

"That's a moan."

"Aha-ha-ha!" She tried again, angrily this time.

"A shout," James said dismissively. He took off his glasses and wiped them on the sleeve of his fleece jacket.

"Haagh-aah-haaaagh!"

Dr. Adam poked his head around the kitchen door. "Can you make less noise, Mandy dear? You're frightening the animals."

Afternoon clinic hours were now well under way.

Mandy glowered across the room. "Blame James. He keeps making me do my cackle."

Dr. Adam couldn't hide a smile. "Is that what it was?"

"Yes. I'm the wicked Witch of the Sea who makes a spell to change the Little Mermaid's fishtail into a pair of legs so she can dance for the human prince she's fallen in love with." Mandy launched into a description of the action.

"Spare me the details, sweetie," her dad cut in. "Your mom and I will be seeing it next week, anyway, so don't spoil it. Gotta run. See you later."

Mandy kept on glowering. "The wicked witch!" she muttered in disgust. "I have to wear a floaty black costumey-thing and a pointy hat."

"A pointy nose and chin?" James chimed in.

"Ha-ha!" She looked in the window at her reflection and made a witch face. "Very funny. Anyway, what about you?" James was one of the prince's courtiers, a minor part that demanded both singing and dancing. "You have to wear a white silk shirt and makeup."

"Don't remind me!" He shuddered. "How did we let ourselves get roped into this?"

Mandy shook her head. "We were in the wrong place at the wrong time." Their music teacher, Mrs. Winterton, had swooped down on them in the biology lab one day after school. They'd stayed behind to clean out Henry the Eighth's cage, and she'd spotted them at the very moment when she was desperate to cast the witch in the play.

"Mandy Hope!" Mrs. Winterton had cried. "You're a confident, outgoing sort of girl, just right for the part." Then she'd turned to James. "And James Hunter, you're perfect for fourth Courtier. Not a big role, but you'll look splendid in the scene where the Mermaid dances for the Prince!"

"You can't say no to Mrs. Winterton," James agreed. "She doesn't give you a chance."

Before they knew it, they'd put Henry the hamster back into his cage and gone to the first rehearsal. That had been six weeks ago. The real performance was next

week, and the music teacher was *still* sighing over
Mandy's cackle.

"Go home this weekend and rehearse a really wicked
laugh," she'd told Mandy. Then she'd turned to James in
near despair. "Mandy's witch isn't evil enough. Lock her
in a room and make her practice. Don't come back to
school on Monday unless she's got it absolutely right!"

"Do it again!" James ordered. They'd been working
for nearly an hour.

"Waagh-haagh-haagh-ha-ha-haagh!" Mandy screeched.

"Got it!" James gasped, fixing his glasses firmly on his
nose and staring at her. "Mandy, that was the most
amazing cackle I've ever heard!"

Rehearsal was over, and Mandy and James decided to
help out at Animal Ark by clearing the snow that had
started to stick in the parking lot. They hurried across
the yard with shovels through the whirling flakes that
blotted out the surrounding hills sloping down toward
Welford Village.

"Uh-oh!" James spotted the round figure of Mrs. Ponsonby as she lifted Pandora, her Pekingese dog, from
the car. Her lively mongrel, Toby, scampered down by
himself and rolled in the snow, his jaws snapping ex-
citedly at it.

"Mandy dear! And James! Could you please help me?"

The fussy older woman struggled to tuck Pandora under one arm and put up her umbrella at the same time.

Mandy ran to hold the umbrella over Pandora, who was wearing a plaid coat over her long cream-colored fur. The dog snuffled and leaned out toward the floating flakes of snow.

"I don't have an appointment," Mrs. Ponsonby explained as she struggled toward the clinic, "but I'm worried about Pandora, so I thought I should bring her in."

"What's wrong with her?" Mandy stumbled alongside, watching James play with Toby in the snow.

The woman shook her head and sighed tragically. "Poor little Pandora is so delicate, and she hates the cold. One can never be too sure."

"But what happened, exactly?" Holding open the clinic door, Mandy glimpsed Jean Knox, the receptionist, filling in forms at the desk. Through the open door of one of the examination rooms, she could see her mom checking the stitches on Bill, a bull terrier that had been in a fight.

Mrs. Ponsonby tossed back her head and stepped inside with the supposedly sick Pekingese. "Pandora *sneezed*! Twice!" she told Jean. "We need to see a vet immediately!"

Two more patients crossed paths with Mrs. Pon-

sonby on their way out of Animal Ark. "Oh, dear, look at the weather!" said Marjorie Spry to her identical twin sister, Joan.

Or was it the other way around? Mandy could never tell the difference between the two sisters. The second twin was carrying their young black-and-white cat, Patch, in a small wire cage.

"How can we drive home in all this snow?" Joan or Marjorie complained at the doorstep.

"Why not leave your car here and let me drive you home, ladies?" David Gill, a farmer from Greystones, was also on his way out. He was tall and steady and took all weather in his long stride. "I have my Land Rover parked outside if you don't mind putting up with the young pig I've got in the back."

As Mrs. Ponsonby sailed forward, demanding attention, and the two nervous women dithered in the doorway, Mandy grinned at James, who was having a snowball fight with Toby in the yard. The dog dodged and barked delightedly.

"A pig?" one of the Miss Sprys fluttered. "Oh, dear! Oh, my!"

"He won't hurt you," Mr. Gill assured her. "And I'll send a farmhand along to get your car when the snow stops. He'll drive you two ladies home, no problem!"

So the twins accepted and took Patch home in the

Land Rover. Meanwhile, Jean explained to Mrs. Ponsonby that Pandora's condition wasn't life threatening and that she must wait her turn in line.

"Line?" Mrs. Ponsonby looked around archly, as if she didn't recognize the word.

There was a row of pet owners sitting quietly with their hamsters, rabbits, cats, and dogs.

"But Pandora *sneezed*!" she repeated, cuddling the dog close to her chest. "It could be pneumonia!"

Jean read down her list for the next appointment. "Joanna Davey and Mabel, the first examination room, please!"

Mandy spied a small white furry creature in a cage. She didn't recognize its owner, a young brown-haired woman in a bright orange fleece jacket and black ski pants. As they went in for a consultation with Dr. Adam, Mandy slipped past Mrs. Ponsonby and around the reception desk into the small, scrubbed examination room. "Can I help?" she whispered to her dad.

Dr. Adam nodded. "Who do we have here?" he asked the newcomer to Welford.

"Mabel. She's a Chinese hamster, expecting babies in about a week." Joanna Davey lifted her pet out of the cage and put her gently on the table. "I noticed she was a bit under the weather when I fed her this morning, and since she's pregnant, I thought I'd better bring her in."

Mandy crouched so that she was at eye level with the table. "Mabel on the table." She smiled to herself. The chubby hamster was pure white, with ruby-red eyes. She squatted on her haunches and clasped her tiny pink forefeet together, close to her nose. Her white whiskers twitched, and her little round ears flicked this way and that.

Dr. Adam examined Mabel from the opposite side of the table, taking her temperature, then looking at her nose, mouth, and eyes. "Yes, she has a runny nose," he observed. "She probably caught a chill in this cold weather."

"Nothing serious?" Joanna asked, gently petting Mabel with her forefinger. The hamster nuzzled against it, then hopped into her cupped hand.

"Probably not. The remedy is to rig up an infrared light on the side of her cage. Turn on the heat, and switch her diet to seeds and water, nothing else. If she's not better in a couple of days, call us." Dr. Adam smiled at the little white creature as she tried, fell back, then succeeded in scrambling up Joanna's arm and onto her shoulder.

Joanna picked her up with the other hand and put her

back in the cage. She'd listened to the brisk, plain instructions. "Anything else?"

"Oh, yes. Do you have other hamsters?"

Joanna Davey nodded. "Two. Honey and Marmalade. A cream-colored satin-coat and a cinnamon angora."

"Well, in that case, keep Mabel isolated from them. You don't want them all sick at the same time." Dr. Adam peeled off his surgical gloves and asked Mandy to wipe down the table with disinfectant. "Remember, if you're at all worried, give us a call."

"Thanks. We're new to Welford, so this is our first visit to Animal Ark." The young woman stood at the door, carrying the hamster cage between both hands. "You've been really helpful. I hope I haven't been too much trouble."

Mandy saw her dad smile, then wince as he overheard Mrs. Ponsonby's loud voice in the waiting room. "Not at all," he assured Joanna Davey. "In fact, you've probably made Mandy's day. She loves hamsters!"

Mandy grinned and blushed. "I'd like to see Honey and Marmalade, too," she confessed.

The young woman grinned back. "Anytime. We moved into a house on the main street in the village, next to the post office."

"Great! Thank you!" Mandy was delighted: Two more hamsters for her to get to know! She loved the small, furry, friendly creatures, with their fat cheek pouches and squat, square bodies.

"Well, how about tomorrow afternoon?" Joanna suggested.

Mandy's eyes lit up, then faded. "I'm sorry, I can't." Rehearsal at school, Sunday afternoon. More cackling.

"She has an appointment with a mermaid," Dr. Adam added jokingly.

"Well, anytime," Joanna said sweetly, turning to go and almost bumping into Mrs. Ponsonby. "Come and see Mabel's babies when they're born. Remember, the house next to the post office — the one with the bright green door." She made her way across the busy waiting room, then paused. "We'll see you soon," she called to Mandy. "Thanks, and bye!"

Two

Sunday dawned cold and crisp.

"The holly and the ivy," Dr. Adam sang, relaxing over the weekend papers. "When they are both full grown . . . *buh-buh-bu-bu-buh* that are in the wood . . ." He blew the tune through puffed-out cheeks.

Mandy giggled. "You look like a hamster!"

"You and hamsters!" he teased. "By the way, Joanna Davey called early this morning to say that the infrared treatment was doing the trick for Mabel. That was nice of her, wasn't it?"

"Yes. I liked her." Mandy was picking up scraps of paper from the windowsill, chairs, and next to the toaster.

14

The papers had lines from the school play written down for her to learn while she went about her routine. There were scraps stuck to the mirror in her bedroom, next to the pony posters on the wall, others on Jean's desk in reception, and one on the back of the bathroom door. "I'll never learn these in time for next Monday." She sighed.

"You will." Dr. Emily appeared at the door, bringing the cold wind in with her. She stamped the snow from her boots and took off her coat. "I've brought in a badger that's been hit by a car," she reported. "Joanna Davey's husband, John, spotted him and flagged me down. I was just on my way back from dropping off that stray hedgehog at Rosa's Refuge."

"A badger!" Mandy gasped. "How is it?"

"Well, he was unconscious at first," her mother replied, "but he came around as I drove him back here. Probably has a concussion from the accident, but I don't think he's broken any bones. I've put him in the residential unit for observation."

Eager to take a look at the badger, Mandy offered to clean the cats' cages in the residential unit while she was there. As she made her way back to the unit, her mom reminded her that in an hour James's dad would arrive to drive her and James over to Walton for their rehearsal.

"And you have to have lunch first!" Dr. Emily called.

But to Mandy the injured badger was much more interesting than lunch. The wild creature lay quietly in a cage usually used for large dogs, his stumpy legs stretched straight out, his coarse gray fur still damp from the melted snow. He heard Mandy approach and raised his head without stirring the rest of his bruised body.

"Poor you!" Mandy put her face close to the cage and gazed in. The badger's flat, black-and-white-striped head sank back onto the blanket. "But we'll look after you now. You'll soon be better, then we'll take you back to where we found you, and you'll be able to make your way back to your nice warm den."

"Sett," Dr. Emily corrected quietly. She had followed Mandy through the back of the cottage into the unit and stood behind her to observe the concussed animal. "Badgers live in setts."

Mandy sighed. "I know. Isn't he gorgeous?"

"Yes. There's something special about badgers," her mother agreed, smiling. "Maybe it's because they're nocturnal, so we hardly ever see them."

"More than that." Mandy backed away to give the patient a chance to rest. "They're strong, and" — she sought for the right word and found it — "secret."

"And quite fierce when necessary," Dr. Emily added,

staying to help Mandy with the cleaning. For a while they talked about badgers' habits in the wild. "I felt when I rescued him from the roadside and brought him back here that it was a privilege to be allowed to help such a magnificent creature," she concluded.

Mandy smiled at her mom. "I think that about every animal that comes to Animal Ark," she confessed.

"I know you do." Dr. Emily smiled back. "That's why you're going to be a great vet when you grow up, Mandy Hope!"

"A better vet than actress," Mandy said glumly a few hours later. "I'll never be able to learn these lines in time." She'd struggled through the first act of the play and retreated to the biology lab to sit with Henry the hamster. Mrs. Winterton was still in the auditorium, with the dancers, including James, going over their steps.

Henry ignored her gloomy predictions. He and Mandy were good friends. She and James had looked after him during one long summer vacation, when they'd put him on a fruit-and-vegetable diet to help the chubby little brown-and-white creature to lose weight. Henry hadn't appreciated their efforts and had promptly escaped into a picnic hamper, where he'd munched his way through a pile of sandwiches and cake.

In fact, the school hamster was good at escaping, though you wouldn't believe it to look at him now. Mandy gazed into the cage on the biology lab shelf as Henry trundled away inside his exercise wheel. His short legs worked furiously, and his shortsighted eyes were fixed firmly ahead as he dedicated himself to keeping fit.

"'I already know what you want!'" Mandy recited her first lines as the Witch of the Sea while gazing at her favorite hamster. The Witch was talking to the Little Mermaid, alias Susan Collins. *(Cackle, cackle.)* "'You want to get rid of your fishtail and have two stumps to walk on like human beings.'" *(Cackle.)* "'It is very unwise of you!'"

"Er, Mandy . . ." James cut into her fourth cackle. He was standing at the door of the lab with small blond Daniel Winterton, the music teacher's seven-year-old son. "I told Daniel he could come and look at Henry."

Mandy continued with her lines. "'You've come just in the nick of time! After tomorrow's sunrise, I could do nothing to help you for another year!'" She laughed again, plucking imaginary toads from her hair and shoulders.

Daniel made a scared face and backed away.

"It's OK," James coaxed. "Don't mind Mandy. Come and see the hamster."

The younger boy sidled into the room after James and crept up to Henry's cage. The class pet trundled happily inside his wheel.

"Daniel was bored," James explained. "He's had to sit through weeks of rehearsal while his mom's been busy with the play. And it just so happens he likes hamsters, don't you, Daniel?"

"I love them." His pale round face had broken into a smile as he watched Henry turn the wheel. "I had one when I was four years old. I called him Norvik. He liked to climb up the curtains. He was a satin-coated Himalayan hamster with red eyes." The smile faded as he spoke.

"What happened to him?" Mandy asked.

"He died." Daniel sighed. "We found him under a pile of wood shavings in the corner of his cage. He probably felt sick while we were at school and crept in there. When we got home, he was dead."

"I'm sorry," Mandy said quietly, gazing over Daniel's shoulder at sturdy, lively Henry and feeling glad that he was healthy. She knew that small pets like hamsters could go downhill very quickly once they grew ill. "Maybe you can get another hamster soon."

Quickly, Daniel Winterton shook his head. "Mom doesn't like hamsters or mice, and because Dad isn't around much to help anymore, she says I'll have to wait until I'm older and able to look after it myself. Anyway, it wouldn't be the same. Norvik was special."

As Daniel's voice trailed off, Henry stopped trundling and hopped out of his wheel. He came to the front of his cage in short, nervous bursts, then poked his little pink nose through the bars.

"He's saying hello." Mandy felt sorry for the sad little boy. She'd noticed him in the auditorium where they rehearsed the play, hidden away in a corner, reading or writing in a notebook he always carried with him. He looked lonely, but Mrs. Winterton seemed too busy to notice.

"Hello," Daniel whispered to Henry, reaching out gently to touch the hamster's nose.

Henry sniffed and sat up on his back legs, front paws dangling, as if begging for food.

"You've had your snack!" Mandy scolded with a smile. She turned to Daniel. "What do you write in your notebook?"

"Stories." He blushed to the roots of his blond hair. "About hamsters. Would you like to see?"

Mandy blinked back her surprise and nodded.

So Daniel brought out his notebook and offered it to Mandy. She took it and opened it to the first page. "The Adventures of Norvik," she read, "by Daniel Winterton. Part One: The Castle on the Hill."

"It's about a hamster that fights to save his family from foxes that live in the castle," Daniel said earnestly, his gray eyes wide and shining. "Norvik is the hero."

Mandy flipped through the pages and read out loud: "'Come back!' the Fox King shouted at his band of cowardly foxes. 'Stay and fight!' He pulled a big, sharp sword from his belt and pointed it at Norvik. 'Prepare to meet your death!'"

"Wow!" James raised his eyebrows. "That's pretty exciting. What happens to Norvik next?"

"He wins the fight," Daniel explained. "Then he rescues his brothers and sisters, then he sets fire to the Fox King's castle, and all the hamsters escape."

"Wow!" It was Mandy's turn to be impressed. She loved the look of the little book, with its clearly printed words and colorful, hand-drawn pictures.

"Daniel! There you are!" Mrs. Winterton bustled into the lab. She was obviously taking a well-earned break from rehearsals and had come looking for her son. She was a thin, pretty woman with thick jet-black hair and big brown eyes, not at all like Daniel. Today she was dressed for action in a long pale blue shirt and black leggings.

"I might have known this was where you'd be!" she exclaimed, noticing Henry in his cage. "Hamsters!" She raised her finely arched eyebrows at Mandy and James. "I can't keep him away."

"Look, Mom, he's saying hello." Daniel pointed to Henry, who was still grabbing the cage wire with his front paws and poking his nose through the gaps.

"Come on, Daniel, I don't have time to look. I've got a million things to do," Mrs. Winterton said. "I want you back in the hall where I can keep an eye on you. And Mandy and James, could you go to the art room for costume fittings with Ms. Temple? You have five minutes before we start on Act Two, so please get going."

"Bye, Henry!" Daniel gave the hamster one last pat.

"You can see him again soon," his mother promised, waiting impatiently by the door. She marched her son down the corridor to the auditorium.

"Be good, Henry," James joked, tickling his stomach through the wire mesh.

The hamster seemed to sigh as he dropped to the floor of his cage and waddled away. Back to the exercise wheel: *squeak, squeak, squeak.*

Mandy took a long last look, smiled, then turned off the light.

"That's good, Mandy!" Mrs. Winterton was happy with her cackle at last.

It was the scene where the mermaid's sisters visited the Witch to plead for her life. The Witch of the Sea drove a hard bargain, telling the sisters that the Little Mermaid must kill her beloved prince in order to save herself. The mermaid sisters did a dance to sad music and sang words that Mrs. Winterton had written herself.

Mandy held up her hands and wiggled her fingers in a scary, witchlike way. She drove the mermaids away with a fierce shriek.

"Very good!" From her seat at the piano, the music teacher praised Mandy's dramatic exit. "Mermaids, you must hold the long notes. And more volume, please. Now, one more time!"

Her part finished for now, Mandy slipped from the stage and made her way across the auditorium. She was looking for Daniel, to ask him more about "The Adventures of Norvik."

"Have you seen Daniel Winterton?" she asked Susan Collins.

The star of the show was busy learning her lines at the back of the room. "Not lately," she murmured, without looking up.

"Try the art room," Vicky Simpson suggested. Vicky was packing away the violin that she played in the school orchestra and taking it down the hall to the music department's storeroom. "Ms. Temple's still in there doing costumes. Maybe Daniel got bored and went with her."

"No, sorry, I haven't seen him," Ms. Temple said when Mandy went to ask. James was standing very still while the biology teacher stuck straight pins into his shirt. It was too big and needed to be taken in.

"Try the biology lab," he suggested. "You know . . . hamster . . . Daniel . . . *ouch!*" One of the pins stuck his arm.

"Don't move!" Ms. Temple ordered.

So Mandy backtracked down the hall to the lab. The light was off, the room in darkness. *Not here, either,* she said to herself. But something made her step inside the door.

It's too quiet! She listened for the squeak of Henry's wheel and heard only silence. *Perhaps he's asleep. No, hamsters come out at night. He should be moving around.* Worried thoughts flashed through her head as she crept across the darkened room, past the long benches where the classes did their practical biology work, toward the shelf where Henry's cage stood. The only light came from the streetlamps in the road outside, which cast a strange orange glare.

"Henry?" Mandy leaned forward to examine the cage.

Nothing. No squeak of the wheel, no curious little brown-and-white face at the bars.

"Henry!" Gripped by real fear, Mandy reached out for the cage door. It swung open at her touch.

"Oh, no!" Swiftly, she looked inside among the piles of wood shavings, under the plastic toy log in one corner, behind the exercise wheel, inside the nest box where the hamster slept. Empty!

Mandy backed off, looking wildly along the shelf. She fell to the floor and scrabbled between the benches and stools. Nothing.

Then she got up and ran for the auditorium. She flew down the big room to the piano where the music teacher was playing. "Please stop, Mrs. Winterton!" she begged, her hair flying across her face, her arms waving in the direction from which she'd come.

"Mandy, what is the matter?" The teacher stood up. Everyone onstage stared at Mandy. Susan and Vicky came forward from the back of the hall. Daniel crept to his mother's side.

"Oh, quick!" she cried. "I need some help. Henry's escaped from his cage. We have to find him!"

Three

"Calm down!" Mrs. Winterton called over the gasps and excited chatter. She got up onto the stage to issue instructions. "Let's all take a break from rehearsal for ten minutes and set up a search party to find the school hamster. Mandy, you take a group back into the biology lab. James, you choose four or five people to help you look along the ground-floor hallways. And Susan, you can cover the art room and the home economics room."

Reluctantly, Susan Collins put down her script. "All this for a hamster!" she grumbled.

"Not just any old hamster," James told her as he gathered his group and headed for the hall. "Henry's a kind of school mascot. We can't let him wander off and get into trouble."

"He might fall off a high shelf," Mandy muttered, "or crawl into one of the ovens in the home economics room." Her imagination was working full tilt. "Hamsters are shortsighted," she explained.

"He might climb inside a cabinet," James added.

"Or into someone's open locker and then get locked in!" Mandy was really panicking now. She noticed Daniel's worried face as he kept close to his mother's side. "Come on, Daniel. You can join our group and help us look."

Daniel frowned and shuffled toward her. "What if Henry manages to get outside?" he whispered.

Mandy shook her head. "Don't even say that! He'll freeze to death. You know how cold it is out there!" The idea sent her running back to the lab. "Let's look under the cabinets," she said to Vicky and her two friends, Claire and Michelle. "Daniel and I will look in Ms. Temple's storeroom."

As they split up to begin a thorough search, the biology teacher came in. "Try not to worry too much," she told the children. "Henry has a habit of escaping, remember. And he always turns up safe and sound."

"The adventures of Henry!" Mandy whispered to Daniel, trying to adopt the biology teacher's more cheerful view. Together they passed the cage and paused to look behind the piles of textbooks next to it. "The bold hamster teetered on the edge of the shelf, staring death in the eye! Panting heavily, he launched himself into midair and plummeted to the ground. Down came the pile of books, crashing after him, pages fluttering in a mysterious wind!"

Daniel refused to smile. His face was shocked and pale. "How did he get out of his cage in the first place?"

Mandy went to the storeroom, opened cabinets, and peered inside. They smelled of rubber tubing and gas from the Bunsen burners stored there. But there was no Henry. "I don't know." Slowly, she turned her head to study Daniel, who was on his hands and knees beside her. His eyes were troubled, so Mandy did her best to cheer him up. "Come on, Henry couldn't get very far," she told him. "He has to be around here somewhere!"

"Any luck?" James put his head around the biology lab door.

Mandy shook her head. They'd been looking for five minutes, and there was no trace of the escapee.

"Me, either." James and his group had searched the entire ground floor. "He's not in the lockers or under the radiators. And I've checked with Susan's group. He's not gobbling ingredients in the home economics room, either."

Henry often headed for food when he made his get-aways. "Is she sure?" Mandy asked doubtfully.

"Yes, I'm sure!" Susan arrived with a toss of her long dark hair. "We've looked in all the drawers and under the stoves. He hasn't even touched the plate of cookies Ms. Temple put out for refreshments earlier this after-noon."

"Hmm." This was unusual. Gingersnaps and choco-late wafers on plates in the room next to the biology lab — a perfect Henry treat. And they were untouched. Henry's sensitive nose must be letting him down.

They were rapidly running out of places to look.

Heavy footsteps plodded down the hallway, and a new face appeared at the biology lab door.

"What's going on?" a deep voice asked. It belonged to Mr. Browning, the school caretaker who kept a careful eye on the site, even on weekends. He was short, stocky, and serious, dressed for the cold weather in a padded jacket, with big woolen socks pulled up over his trousers, and sturdy walking boots.

"It's the hamster," Mrs. Winterton explained, drifting by with a frazzled expression on her face as she headed for the music department storeroom, music scores and a clarinet tucked under her arm. She disappeared inside and could be heard moving heavy instruments around in the small space.

"Don't tell me he's escaped again?" Mr. Browning tutted and frowned at Mandy as if it must be her fault.

"I'm afraid so." Ms. Temple emerged from the art room and stepped in to keep the peace. "But don't worry, Mr. Browning, Henry will turn up."

"Hmph!" The caretaker pressed his thin lips together. "Well, he'd better put in an appearance pretty fast," he warned. "I'm not keeping the school open after four o'clock. That's all I'm getting paid for. Anyhow, I have my last-minute Christmas shopping to do. So in three-quarters of an hour I chuck you all out and lock up for the night."

Grumpily, he swung his large bunch of keys at them, turned, and stomped off down the hall.

"Thanks for nothing!" James murmured under his breath.

Just then, Mrs. Winterton reappeared. "Er . . . Mandy, James!" she whispered, edging backward into the hallway.

"Is it Henry?" James sprang forward.

"In here!" The music teacher held her finger to her lips to warn them to be quiet. "At least, I think so!"

Mandy ran to follow James. "Come on, Daniel!" The three of them crowded around Mrs. Winterton.

"Look on top of the drums," the teacher whispered.

Sure enough, they could hear sharp little feet running over the taut surface of the bass drum. *Rat-a-tat-tat! Swish, thump!* Henry skidded against the rim of the drum. He peered over the edge with a bewildered expression on his furry face.

"Thank goodness!" Mandy breathed a sigh of relief and edged into the cramped, airless room. "Get his cage, Daniel."

As the little boy ran to do as he was asked, his mother conferred with Mandy and James. "I'm not too eager to be in the same room with anything like a hamster," she confessed. She seemed out of breath and nervous. "Mice, guinea pigs, rats — they all make me feel uneasy. I used to leave the animal care to my husband when Daniel had his pet hamster. Is it all right if I leave you two to persuade Henry to get back into his cage while I take the other members of the cast to the auditorium and continue with our rehearsal?"

"Of course." James was so relieved to see Henry, he wouldn't take his eyes off him as the hamster poised on the edge of the bass drum, ready to launch himself onto a nearby cymbal.

"Good," said Mrs. Winterton, relaxing slightly. "Join us as soon as you can. We have to go through the finale before we leave — and you know what Mr. Browning's like. He'll want us out on the dot!" She made a hasty retreat.

Crash! Henry landed on the metal disk and clung on. Slowly, he slipped toward the edge.

"Uh-oh!" Mandy dived across the room to catch him, tripped over a cello case, and missed.

Henry dropped from the cymbal onto a keyboard and scurried along the polished white keys.

"Henry was on a narrow ledge." James laughed and told the hero's story. "Below him, a grisly, giant face cried out in pain. He knew that he had only seconds to escape from the monster's horrible grasp!"

"Ha-ha!" Mandy rubbed her bruised elbows and got up. By now, Daniel had arrived with the hamster cage. James shut the door behind him. At least now there was no way out for Henry. Meanwhile, the runaway pet had jumped off the keyboard and scurried along the table, behind a shiny French horn.

"He's vanished!" Daniel cried.

Mandy was nearest, so she reached across guitar cases to look behind the horn. "Gone!" she reported.

"Impossible!" James climbed over two double basses and a loudspeaker to join her.

"He has — he's vanished!" Mandy tried to think straight. She began to scour the area, looking behind clarinets and trumpets and inside empty instrument cases to see if Henry had sneaked in anywhere.

"There are so many places he could hide!" James complained.

"And we thought we were so close to cornering him!"

"We still are," Mandy insisted. The door was closed. There were no windows for Henry to climb through. "If we split up and take one section of the room each, we're bound to find him."

So Daniel put the empty cage near the door and joined in. For fifteen minutes, they carefully lifted and moved every single instrument in the storeroom.

"Nothing!" James sighed.

Mandy stood up and eased her stiff back. Some of the bigger instruments like the cellos and double basses were heavy.

Just then, there was a knock at the door. "Mandy! James! Mrs. Winterton says you have to come and rehearse the finale!" It was Susan's voice.

"Tell her we haven't found Henry yet," Mandy pleaded. Her face was red and shiny from the effort of shifting the instruments.

"She says to leave Daniel to continue looking while you two do your parts onstage. You can come back in five minutes!"

Mandy sighed.

"OK. Daniel, you heard her: We'll be back in five minutes!"

Reluctantly, they opened the door a crack, squeezed through, then shot off to the auditorium. They went onstage and walked through their parts in the final song, hardly noticing what they were doing.

"Courtiers, come forward and take your bow!" Mrs. Winterton ordered.

James and three other boys did as they were told. Then James slid away, back to the storeroom.

"Witch of the Sea, come forward!" Mrs. Winterton played the Witch's theme music.

Mandy bowed and escaped after James.

"Daniel, are you there?" James had run down the hall and was knocking at the door when Mandy joined him.

"Yes," a muffled voice answered.

"Have you found Henry?"

There was a long pause, then, "No!"

Mandy and James groaned.

"OK, let us in again, quick!" James had spotted the caretaker striding down the hallway, looking at his watch.

"We have to get Henry back before he locks up," Mandy hissed, hearing the jangle of keys. "If we leave him loose, anything could happen before school opens again tomorrow morning!" The situation was getting serious, despite what Ms. Temple had said earlier.

"Don't tell me!" James leaned against the door, waiting for Daniel to open it the fraction they needed to get back inside.

"I want to come out!" The small boy's face appeared at the crack. "I don't like it in here by myself!"

"OK!" James was just about to slip in instead when Mr. Browning approached him and Mandy.

"Is that hamster still loose?" the caretaker demanded, keys jingling in his pocket. "You know it's five minutes to four."

"We just need a little more time," Mandy begged.

He shook his head. "Sorry. No can do." He walked on, checking rooms right and left.

"We've got four minutes." Mandy sighed.

"Let me out!" Daniel said again.

"OK, we're ready," James told him. "Are you sure Henry's nowhere near the door?"

"I told you, no! I haven't found him!" He sounded as if he was almost in tears.

So James eased open the door. Daniel came out hanging his head, carefully carrying a black violin case, and shuffled off down the hallway.

James slipped into the stuffy room to take his place, but Mandy hesitated before following him. "Hang on, Daniel," she called.

The little boy didn't stop, so Mandy ran after him. "Where are you taking that violin?" she asked.

"Home," he muttered.

"What for?" Mandy's suspicions grew. Daniel was behaving very strangely, refusing to look up or to stop.

"Mom says I have to practice."

"I didn't know you played the violin." She stepped in front of him. "Anyway, when will you have time to practice before tomorrow?"

"Tonight," he said angrily, glaring up at her. Pulling the case up in front of him, he tried to sidestep past Mandy. The clumsy movement made him almost drop the case. He caught it as it slipped, but the catch clicked, and the lid swung open. Inside, it was empty.

Or was it? Daniel gave a frightened cry and desperately tried to close the case, but Mandy had seen a movement. A brown-and-white shape scuttled across the blue velvet interior.

"Henry!" The hamster was inside the violin case!

James heard Mandy's cry and came running, followed

by Ms. Temple, then Mr. Browning, tramping back down the hall to see what all the fuss was about.

Daniel Winterton froze on the spot. His gray eyes filled with tears, his bottom lip trembled. There was no room for doubt: Mandy had caught him red-handed, trying to sneak Henry out of the school.

Four

"Oh, Daniel!" Mrs. Winterton's face trembled with disappointment. "How could you even think of stealing poor Henry?"

Tears spilled out of the little boy's eyes and slid down his round cheeks. "I just really, really wanted to look after him!" he cried.

"But what would you have done with him if you'd managed to get him out of school?" Mandy asked.

They'd gathered in the biology lab: Daniel and his mother, Ms. Temple, James, and Mandy. Everyone else was being shown out of the building by an impatient Mr. Browning. Henry was back in his cage, safe and sound.

"I would've kept him secret and put him in Norvik's old cage," Daniel explained miserably. "He would've been my very own pet."

"But how?" James's logical mind ran ahead. "Your mom would have found out. Henry's a real live animal; he needs food and water. You'd have to clean out his cage and spend lots of time talking to him so he didn't get lonely."

"Ah!" Mrs. Winterton sighed. "I think you might have hit on something there," she told James. "About pets not being allowed to get lonely. I'm afraid it's Daniel who's been the lonely one lately."

The little boy hung his head and sniffed.

"You see, his daddy's been working in London since September. He comes home for weekends, and he'll be back for Christmas, but Daniel misses him a lot. And I've been so busy with the school play that I haven't been able to spend much time with Daniel, either."

Mandy nodded. She felt sorry for the shy, bookish boy and tried to imagine what it would be like if her own dad worked away from home. "It's not long till Christmas," she reminded him.

"But, Daniel, the fact remains that you shouldn't have tried to trick Mandy and James into thinking that you hadn't found Henry," Mrs. Winterton explained. "Think how unhappy they would have been if they'd gone home believing that the school hamster was lost for good!" His mother was still disappointed in him.

"And Henry already has a nice, cozy home," Ms. Temple added, "except for the loose catch on the cage door." She took a screwdriver from a drawer and tightened the screws holding the catch in place. "I'm fixing it so it won't come loose again," she told Mandy and James. "That's what must have happened before, without anyone noticing, and smart little Henry was quick to take advantage when our backs were turned."

"At least everything worked out OK," James said, hearing Mr. Browning's footsteps stamping down the hallway. "The adventures of Henry have ended happily once again!"

"I think this lump on Tiddles's eyelid has been caused by hedgehog ticks." Dr. Emily was busy in the clinic when Mandy arrived home from school late on Monday afternoon.

After the latest nerve-racking rehearsal for the school play, Mandy had slipped into the residential unit to reassure herself that the badger with the concussion was well on the road to recovery, then gone into the examination room to see her mom in action.

Dr. Emily was bending over Ernie Bell's cat while the old man stood to one side. Despite his frowning manner, Ernie was softhearted toward Tiddles and his pet squirrel, Sammy.

"Is it serious?" he asked, too anxious to look around and say hello to Mandy.

"Her ears and eyelids are covered with the ticks," she explained. "I take it Tiddles still spends a fair amount of time outside?"

"I can't keep her in." The elderly man shook his head. "She's a wanderer, always out and about."

Ernie's house was in the center of the village, next to the Fox and Goose, where there were plenty of chances for Tiddles to mix with other cats.

"Well, she's been unlucky. The ticks are parasites, and they've decided that Tiddles is a good host now that any sensible hedgehog is hibernating for the winter." Dr. Emily dabbed at the lump above the cat's eye with a cotton swab. "What's probably happened is that Tiddles has scratched at a tick. The tiny wound has become infected and caused the eyelid to swell."

Mandy put down her schoolbag as she listened to the description. Tiddles was one of the kittens she and James had found homes for after Walton, the school cat, had given birth to them in the former caretaker's kitchen.

"I'll give you some antibiotic to crush and put in Tiddles's food and some spray to deal with the ticks. The problem should clear up within the next few days." Dr. Emily lifted the young cat and handed her back to her owner.

The cat's owner smiled with relief as he held his squirming pet. "I'm thankful it's nothing worse. You hear that, Mandy?" He turned and nodded. "Your mom's a clever lady. She knows her stuff."

Mandy grinned back, glad that Ernie was happy. His lined, sharp-featured face had creased into deep wrinkles so that his eyes almost disappeared beneath his bushy white eyebrows. As he and Tiddles went out, she helped her mom wipe down the examination table.

"Good rehearsal?" Dr. Emily asked, peeling off her surgical gloves. Tiddles had been her last patient of the day. She unbuttoned her white coat and led the way into reception, where Jean Knox was finishing work.

"Awful!" Mandy groaned. "Mrs. Winterton says we have to stay after school every day this week, *and* go in on Saturday and Sunday afternoon!"

"It'll all be worthwhile," her mom promised. "Once you get up there on that stage in front of a real audience, I'm sure you'll enjoy it."

"Ohhhh!" Mandy grimaced. "Don't, Mom!" The thought of a real audience terrified her.

"I'll be there," Jean promised, folding her glasses and

putting them in their case. "I have a seat in the front row."

"Uhhh!" Mandy sagged against the desk.

"And all of Welford will be there, too!" Jean's eyes twinkled. "The Walton school play is part of our tradition. No one wants to miss it."

"We've bought our tickets already," Dr. Emily reminded Mandy. "So have Gran and Grandpa."

"I hope it snows and everyone gets stuck inside their houses!" Mandy exclaimed. She sank farther down, longing for the bad weather to return. Since Saturday, the snow had melted, except on top of the hills. "Then they'd have to call the whole thing off!"

Dr. Adam overheard her as he came out of the second examination room. "The holly and the ivy . . . when they are both full grown . . . *buh-buh-bu-bu-buh-bu-bu* in the wood . . ."

"I'm serious, Dad!" No one seemed to understand how bad stage fright felt. In exactly a week's time, on Monday the twenty-first of December, Mandy would have to put on her witch clothes and pointy hat to go onstage in front of hundreds of people and cackle for real!

The week sped by, and Mrs. Winterton was putting on the pressure to get the show ready for Monday while

Ms. Temple dashed here and there with costumes and props under her arms. There wasn't even five minutes to spare for Mandy to visit Honey and Marmalade at the Daveys' new house. Then, at home, on Wednesday evening, Mandy's mom and dad decided that the badger was well enough to be returned to the wild.

"Would you like to come?" Dr. Emily asked her daughter.

Mandy looked up from her homework and out the kitchen window at a clear, starry sky. She nodded eagerly.

"Get well bundled up, then. I'll bring the badger out to the car and meet you there."

Mandy ran upstairs for her warmest sweater. In five minutes, she was ready and waiting in the frosty yard.

"Watch out! He's pretty impatient." Dr. Emily lifted the cage with the badger into the back of the car. The sturdy creature turned swiftly in small circles, sniffing the fresh night air with his long black snout. Once in the car, he came to the front of the cage and pressed his nose against the wire mesh, his small eyes gleaming.

"Where are we going to set him free?" Mandy asked. She felt a small knot of excitement in her stomach as they left Animal Ark and drove carefully down the narrow road toward the village. The headlights of the four-wheel-drive car showed every blade of stiff, frost-covered grass and the tangled bramble branches on either side of the road.

"You know the post office?" Dr. Emily stopped at the intersection of the main street to wait for two cars and a motorcycle to pass. "There's a gap at the side of the building between the post office and the row of houses where the Daveys have just moved in."

"I know where you mean." Mandy glanced over her shoulder to check on the badger. The scared creature had retreated to a corner of the cage, unable to make sense of the swaying, jolting movement of the Land Rover. He thrust his nose forward and craned his neck toward the fresh air coming in through the slightly open window.

"I'm guessing that he came down through that gap when he was hit. There are fields at the back of the houses, and then a small grove — just the sort of territory where a badger would make his sett."

"So we'll take him down the alley and set him free in the field?" Mandy understood the plan.

"Yes. Then I thought we might stop in at the Daveys," Dr. Emily continued as she pulled up and parked by the telephone booth outside the post office.

"To see Mabel?" Mandy jumped out and ran around the back to open the door. She began to pull the badger's heavy cage toward her.

Her mom came to lend a hand. Together they lifted and carried the cage, Dr. Emily walking backward, Mandy guiding her across the sidewalk and down the narrow alley beside the stone post office. "Yes, to see how Mabel's pregnancy is going," Dr. Emily said. "And to see Marmalade and —"

"Honey!" Mandy finished. "Careful! There's a patch of ice ahead."

They skirted around the dangerous frozen puddle and walked on. Mandy's arms were aching, and the badger was turning anxiously inside the small space. His weight rocked the cage and made it more difficult to handle. In spite of the freezing cold, Mandy began to feel hot inside her thick sweater, jeans, boots, and jacket.

"Almost there," Dr. Emily said.

At last they reached the gate into the field and put the cage on the ground.

Mandy looked around. "Watch out, there's someone coming!" she whispered. She could see in the moonlight that a solitary figure was crossing the frozen field.

"It's all right, it's only me!" The man waved and kept coming. "I'm heading for my midweek visit to the Fox and Goose."

"Hello, David!" Dr. Emily recognized the tall figure of David Gill, the owner of Greystones Farm. The far border of his land touched the grove of trees where they planned to release the badger. She told him the plan and asked his advice. "Are we doing the right thing, releasing the badger on his original home turf?"

"Absolutely right," David Gill agreed. "He'll soon chase off any other creatures like foxes that might have moved in while he's been laid up in the hospital, so to speak. Before you know it, it'll be business as usual for him."

Mandy listened eagerly. "Shall I let him out now?"

"Just wait for him to get his bearings." Opening the wide gate into the field, the farmer explained that the badger would soon recognize where he was by familiar sounds and smells. After a few minutes standing in a cold wind, blowing into their cupped hands and hugging themselves to keep warm, he said it was safe to open the door.

Mandy stooped and fumbled at the catch with her cold fingers. It clicked. The door swung open on its hinges, and she stood back.

Cautiously, the badger crept forward. At the edge of the cage he lowered his head and sniffed at the ground. He took one step out, then another, raising his head to look at the moon and stars: listening, watching.

"Go on!" Mandy urged him away from the road toward the open field. The knot in her stomach tightened.

The stripe of white along the sturdy creature's head showed clearly in the dim light. There was a gleam in his black eyes. Slowly, he put his nose to the ground and snuffled toward the gate. His heavy paws crackled on the frosty grass. Then, with a sudden flurry and a push from his strong back legs, he was off.

Across the field, making a dark track through the white frost, the badger ran, silent, fast, and low. He brushed past high tufts of frozen grass and weeds, zig-zagging past brambles until he reached the bare haw-thorn hedge by the wood. Then he stopped to look over his shoulder to where David Gill, Mandy, and her mom still stood. There was a flash of white fur as he turned his head. Then he dipped low and crept through a break in the spiked branches, vanishing into the darkness.

"What did I tell you?" Mr. Gill nodded and gave a sat-isfied grunt. "He'll be just fine. And I'll get my boy, Bran-don, to check the sett every so often, just to make sure."

Mandy smiled and sighed. She felt relieved and sad as the badger disappeared.

"Come on," her mom said quietly. "Let's go and see if the Daveys will give us a nice mug of hot chocolate."

"Meet Marmalade, the cinnamon-colored angora!" Jo-anna Davey introduced Mandy to a beautiful, silky-

haired, bright orange creature. She held him in the palm of one hand, turned him on his back, and tickled his white tummy.

"And this is Honey, the cream satin-coat." John Davey showed her a trimmer, sleeker, pale-fawn hamster with big dark eyes.

Mandy was thrilled to be handling the two adorable creatures at long last. They were every bit as sweet as she'd imagined during the long, nerve-racking rehearsals for the play.

"She and Marmalade are staying in the living room while Mabel's been ill," Mr. Davey continued. "They love the warmth from the fire, and now we don't have the heart to move them back to the breakfast room again."

John was obviously as keen on keeping fit as his athletic-looking wife. He wore jogging pants and sneakers, with a bright red sweatshirt. His medium-brown hair was cut short, and his face glowed as if he'd just come back from a run.

"Would you like to hold Honey?" he asked Mandy.

She took the tiny creature and felt the hard claws and long, soft whiskers tickle her palm. She cupped her hands carefully, scared that Honey would take fright at being held by a stranger and try to jump to freedom.

Meanwhile, Dr. Emily was telling Joanna about the

safe return of the badger to the wild. "We fed him well while we had him at Animal Ark," she told her, "so he's laid down a couple of layers of fat as protection against the cold. We're hoping he'll find his old sett and be able to bed down there until the frost thaws."

"The forecast is for snow this weekend," Joanna reported.

"Good!" Mandy said.

"Are you hoping for a white Christmas?" John said, taking Honey back and putting her into her small plastic cage.

"No. I'm hoping they'll cancel the school play!" She explained about being forced into being the Witch of the Sea.

"We've bought tickets for that," their new friend protested. "We thought we'd go to the show as a way of getting to meet people."

"We'll see you there, then." Dr. Emily watched Joanna return Marmalade to his cozy bed of wood shavings. Then they all went to the breakfast room to look at Mabel.

"All's well," said John.

The grown-ups chatted while Mandy concentrated on Mabel, who looked cheerful and perky after her recent slight chill. The tubby, obviously pregnant white hamster was chewing at a dish of sunflower and sesame seeds, stuffing the food into her cheek pouches and glancing warily at Mandy all the while.

Dr. Emily joined Mandy to cast an expert eye over the patient. "How's the mom-to-be?" she asked.

"Thriving now." John gave an update. "Her babies are due on Saturday or Sunday, which is why I was a little cautious about coming to the show on Monday night. It will depend on whether Mabel gives birth on the right day. If not, we might have to stick around to keep an eye on her."

"Or you could go to the show, and I could stay with the hamster," Joanna suggested. She had gone to the kitchen to put up a pot of water.

"We'll see."

Once more, Mandy let the conversation flow over her. She sat with her elbows on the table, watching Mabel pick at the seeds with her delicate paws, turning them this way and that, then stuffing them into her mouth. She thought of the badger rooting through the frosty undergrowth, announcing his return to the area with gruff barks and strong scents, scaring off any small creature that might have crept into his warm, well-built sett while he'd been away.

"Mandy?" Her mom's voice broke in.

"Mmm?" Mabel had finished her supper and was rest-ing in her dark, warm nest box. Mandy was gazing sleepily at what looked like an empty cage.

"Time to go."

They said good-bye to the Daveys and drove home. Snowflakes began to drift across the headlight beams.

"Tired?" Dr. Emily asked gently.

"Mmm." Mandy nodded. "Mabel's sweet. And so are Honey and Marmalade."

"The play will soon be over," her mom added sympathetically, turning carefully into the driveway at Animal Ark. The lights in the house were on, casting a warm glow. There was a sprinkling of snow on the yard. "And then it'll be Christmas, and we can all relax!"

Five

"Still nervous?" Dr. Adam asked Mandy as he pulled up outside the school on the Monday evening of the last week of the semester.

"Terrified," she admitted.

The big night had arrived, but not the hoped-for snow. In fact, the weather had been cold and clear for days and, though a deep frost had set in, there wasn't a snow cloud to be seen.

Members of *The Little Mermaid* cast and musicians in the Walton School orchestra had been able to travel freely to rehearsals from the villages and farms. The

play had come together in a last frantic scramble of costume sewing, scenery painting, and prop making, so
that by the end of Sunday afternoon even Mrs. Winterton was satisfied that the show was going to be a success.

"Remember, everyone, our school has a great tradition of excellent plays to keep up!" On Sunday, she'd
made a final speech before they'd all gone home. "I
know the orchestra will perform well, and every actor
will try to be word perfect. Singers and dancers, don't
let me down. I know you can all do it, each and every
one of you!" The dark-haired director had tried to be encouraging.

Daniel Winterton had sat at the back of the hall as
usual. All week, since Henry had ended his adventures
inside the empty violin case, the little boy had kept in
the background. Mandy had found him hunched in cor-
ners over another of his red notebooks. She had asked
to look at his story and tried to be kind, but Daniel had
shaken his head and turned his back. Once or twice,
she'd found him in the biology lab, drawing pictures of
Henry and sticking them in his book. But when he noticed her, Daniel slipped out without a word.

"I bet Daniel will be glad when the show's over,"
James had said as they all trooped out of school on Sun-

day evening. The dress rehearsal had been long and tiring. He, too, had noticed how unhappy the little boy was.

"He's not the only one." Mandy had sighed. "You know something? I'd rather have a week of nonstop math quizzes than be in this play!"

"I'd rather . . . walk a tightrope across Niagara Falls!" James had declared.

"Or get stuck in an elevator with . . . Mrs. Ponsonby!" Mandy struggled to invent fates worse than death.

"What's that about our dear Mrs. P?" Dr. Adam had asked, holding open the Land Rover's door for James and Mandy to climb in.

"Nothing!" they'd said together, sinking back into the seats.

But neither Mandy nor James slept a wink that night, and all day at school, the tension mounted.

"I wish I could make time stand still!" James had whispered to Mandy when he'd seen her in the hall at lunchtime.

"Maybe we could break an arm or a leg!" She'd suggested the rash solution after school while they waited for the bus to take them home to Welford. "Then we wouldn't be able to be in the play."

But their sensible moms had an early supper prepared and made sure they were ready for the big night.

"Good luck!" Dr. Emily had called from the doorstep of Animal Ark, as a pale-faced, trembling Mandy set off back to school. "I'll see you later!"

Dr. Adam had picked up James and driven them over the moor, and now here they were, standing in the school entrance with dozens of other nervous actors, musicians, and dancers. "Watch out, here comes the boss!" he murmured with a grin as Mrs. Winterton strode across the parking lot, trailing Daniel after her. The music teacher looked as nervous and on edge as any member of her cast.

"Not now, Daniel!" she insisted.

"But, Mo-om!" It seemed to Mandy that he'd been pestering for some time. His voice was whining and pathetic; his mother's mouth was set in a firm line. "Why can't I have another hamster? You said I could have a treat if I was good. And I have been, haven't I? I've been really, really quiet, and I haven't gotten in your way at all this week!"

Trotting in his mother's footsteps, the little boy didn't seem to realize that he'd chosen the worst possible moment to ask. Mandy felt sorry for him and shrugged her shoulders at her dad and James. Then they all stood to one side as Mrs. Winterton swept by.

"And I *will* look after it, I promise! I'll feed it and clean its cage and make sure it gets plenty of exercise!"

Mrs. Winterton stopped inside the porch, clutching her music scores and bending forward to hiss in his ear. "Daniel, will you listen to me? I'm very, very busy right now. The last thing I want to think about is whether or not you can keep another smelly little hamster in the house!"

"Hamsters aren't smelly," he protested stubbornly, staring up at her without blinking. "And you said I could choose my favorite treat!"

"But *not* a hamster!" She put her face close to his. Their noses were only inches apart, Daniel's eyes wide and blank, his mother's blazing with frustration. "Do you understand? I'm busy. I'm trying to put on a show!"

Dr. Adam cleared his throat and stepped forward. "Would you like me to take Daniel out for a little while?" he offered.

"Aha!" Mrs. Winterton seized his arm. "Now, Daniel, Mandy's father is a vet. He'll tell you exactly why we can't have another hamster, then that will be the end of it!"

"I will?" Dr. Adam looked surprised.

"Yes, tell him that they take an awful lot of looking after."

"Er . . . as a matter of fact . . ."

Mandy listened to her dad stammer. Mrs. Winterton was determined to have her say.

"And anyway, Daniel, remember what it was like when Norvik died!" She turned to Dr. Adam. "To be honest, I didn't really have anything to do with the creature. I don't like rodents, so Daniel's father took care of it. But Daniel doted on it. He was absolutely heartbroken when we lost it and cried for days."

"It can be a very upsetting experience," Dr. Adam admitted thoughtfully.

"He moped and moped," Daniel's mother continued, "and then he started drawing all these hamster pictures. Really, I was very worried about him for weeks afterward!"

"But Dad isn't away *all* of the time," Daniel muttered. "If we got another hamster, he could help me look after him again. And anyway, I'm older. I can do it myself now."

His mother shook her head. "You see what I mean!" She appealed to Mandy's father. "He's obsessed with hamsters."

"Let me look after him for half an hour," Dr. Adam offered again. "I have to drive back to Welford to pick up Mandy's mother and grandparents. Daniel could come along for the ride."

The music teacher looked at her watch and nodded. "Thanks. That would be nice, wouldn't it, Daniel?"

"Hmm," the boy grunted, then looked away, out at the

frost-covered parking lot and the row of holly trees beyond.

Dr. Adam shrugged at Mandy and wished her and James luck before they rushed off to get ready for the show. "Knock 'em dead!" he said with a wink.

Mandy swallowed hard. Her throat was already dry, her palms sticky, and there was still an hour to go before the curtain went up.

"And Daniel, before we go on our drive, why don't you take me to see the school hamster?" Dr. Adam spoke casually but gave Mrs. Winterton a serious look. "You could show me how Henry's doing, couldn't you?"

Daniel's face lit up at the word "hamster." He glowed when he heard Dr. Adam say Henry's name.

But Mrs. Winterton didn't like the idea. "No," she said with a firm shake of her head. "I'd rather you didn't encourage him."

So Dr. Adam swiftly changed his tack. "OK, then. Daniel, are you ready to go now?"

The little boy stared at the floor in silence.

"Daniel?" his mother prompted.

"Yes," said a small, flat voice. Daniel hung his head as Dr. Adam explained that they would be back in time for the show.

"So, Mandy, get going," Mrs. Winterton ordered, noticing her hovering nearby. "I want everyone in costume by seven o'clock. That gives you exactly twenty minutes to get changed and made up. And you, James, hurry up! There isn't a moment to lose!"

The first-floor room where the cast changed into their costumes overlooked the school's main entrance. Mandy dashed up there in time to see her dad and Daniel driving out of the grounds past the row of tall holly trees. She sighed, then went to find Ms. Temple, who gave her the flowing black costume and tall witch's hat.

"I want you to wear these for the actual performance," the biology teacher told her, handing Mandy a set of small, greenish plastic objects. "They're Halloween witch's fingernails — just right for the part."

Mandy stuck one on the end of each finger and wiggled them. Now her hands really did look witchlike.

"And you didn't have full green makeup on for the dress rehearsal, did you?" Ms. Temple sat Mandy down on a stool and slapped on the cold, oily-smelling theater makeup. "And wrinkles." A black eyebrow pencil made lines between Mandy's eyes and down the sides of her mouth.

Mandy held still while the teacher worked. At the end of the session, when she looked in the mirror and saw her blacked-out front teeth and wispy gray wig under the tall hat, she hardly recognized herself.

"Now, wait quietly for the curtain to go up," Ms. Temple told her, moving on to Susan Collins. "And don't smudge your wrinkles!"

Mandy raised her arms and wriggled her fingers in front of the mirror. She mimed a cackle. *Hmm, not bad.* She twirled around in her floating, flowing black cape. *Not bad at all.* "Like my fingernails?" she asked James, who had just changed into his courtier's costume.

"Mandy?" He stared at her doubtfully.

"Yes, it's me!" She gave a toothless grin.

"Hey!" he said, obviously impressed.

Then she went to look out the window at the cars arriving for the show, wondering if her dad had come back with her mom and her grandparents.

James followed. "Here come Simon and Jean," he pointed out.

Simon was the young nurse at Animal Ark, and he'd given the receptionist a lift from Welford. The two of them walked together to join a steady flow into the building.

"And Mr. and Mrs. Collins." Mandy pointed out a sleek, shiny car. Getting out were Susan's glamorous actress-mother and tall, good-looking father. Mrs. Collins was wrapped in a warm fur coat, with a white silk scarf thrown across one shoulder. "I hope that fur's fake," Mandy grumbled, enjoying her bird's-eye view.

"Of course it is!" Susan said, passing by. She was wearing her long mermaid's wig and tight, shiny fishtail, taking tiny steps across the room. "Mommy wouldn't wear real fur!"

"That was Susan Collins!" Mandy mouthed at James, in case he hadn't recognized the star of the show.

"I know!" He pointed out more new arrivals. "Ernie Bell and Walter Pickard . . . Mrs. Ponsonby with Marjorie and Joan Spry . . ."

Mandy glanced down at the three women. Mrs. Ponsonby was dressed in a red cape and hat. She carried Pandora under one arm and held Toby's leash with the other hand. She was stopped at the door by Mr. Browning, who seemed to be explaining that dogs weren't allowed in the school building. Mrs. Ponsonby protested. The caretaker stood firm. So while the Spry twins went in to take their seats in the hall, a fuming Mrs. Ponsonby was forced to take her precious pets back to the car.

"I hope they're going to be warm enough." Mandy watched closely as Mrs. Ponsonby settled them down in a nest of blankets in the back of her car, which was parked in the shelter of the holly bushes. She opened a window for fresh air and wagged her finger at Toby to warn him to be good. Then, satisfied that the dogs would be all right, she bustled back toward the main entrance.

"Five minutes to go!" James looked at the clock above the door.

Mandy's stomach lurched. She was trying not to think about curtain time.

"Here come the McKays." James had spotted his Welford neighbors, Dr. and Mrs. McKay and their daughter, Claire. They ran Rosa's Refuge, the hedgehog sanctuary, from the backyard of their large house. People were arriving thick and fast. "Three minutes!" he murmured.

Mandy felt her skin begin to prickle. Sweat formed under the thick layer of makeup. "I'm going to melt!" she groaned. Suddenly, she panicked. "Where's Dad?" All of Welford seemed to be here, except for her family.

"Would all members of the orchestra please take their places!" Mrs. Winterton called from the dressing-room door. Her voice was high and tense as the big moment drew near.

The room emptied as the musicians took their instruments and filed downstairs.

"And all actors and dancers for the opening scene, please make your way backstage!" The music teacher checked their costumes as they passed. "You look lovely, Susan!" She tweaked the mermaid's wig and shiny fish scales, then sent her on her way.

"Mandy, I have to go. Are you OK?" James asked.

"Yep." She gazed anxiously out the window. Her first appearance wasn't until Scene Two.

"If you're worried about your dad, I'm sure he'll turn up." He was reluctant to leave, but Mrs. Winterton was waiting impatiently at the door. "See you later."

"Good luck!" she told him absentmindedly. Where could her family be? Would they all miss the beginning of the show?

"You, too," James murmured, leaving her alone.

All this, and Mom, Dad, Gran, and Grandpa might not even be here to see her! Mandy tried not to let disappointment get the better of her. *There must be a good reason*, she told herself. *They've just been held up for a little while. They'll be here soon.*

Gazing out the window and down at the rows of parked cars, she saw nothing but the shadows of the holly trees falling long and silent across the frost-covered driveway.

Six

"Hello up there!" A faint call from the parking lot distracted Mandy's attention from the silent trees. "Witch of the Sea — Mandy Hope! Hello!"

It was her gran, standing by the Animal Ark Land Rover, which had just driven into the school grounds. She was waving her arms and smiling up at Mandy, who opened the window and leaned out. "You're here!" she cried.

"Sorry we're late, dear. The show hasn't started yet, has it?" Dorothy Hope stepped to one side to let Mandy's grandpa, Dr. Emily, and Daniel Winterton out

68

of the car. The grown-ups looked flustered, but Daniel was beaming all over.

"Not quite." Mandy glanced up at the clock. "One minute to go!"

"There was a small crisis at the Daveys' house on our way here. I wonder, is there any room at the inn for two unexpected visitors?" Gran called.

Mystified, Mandy leaned still farther out. "What do you mean?"

"Come and see!" Dorothy Hope beckoned her down.

"Can I, please?" Mandy turned to ask Ms. Temple, who had joined her at the window. Apart from the two of them, the room was empty.

"Let's both go," the teacher decided promptly, taking in the situation and heading for the door. "We'll use the back stairs, so no latecomers will see you in costume."

They slipped quickly along the hall, down to the ground floor, past the art room, and into Ms. Temple's biology lab.

Mandy flew across the room ahead of the teacher, her black robes billowing behind her. Out of the corner of her eye, she glimpsed Henry in his cage. The hamster was sitting quietly at his food dish. Mandy pushed open the side door that led to the sloping path and was greeted by a blast of freezing cold air.

Quickly, she and Ms. Temple ran up the frosty path, Mandy knocking snow off the holly trees and brushing against low branches as she rushed by. The snow slid from the shiny leaves and fell with a soft thud.

"Mandy, there you are! That's a marvelous costume, dear!" Gran greeted her as she rounded the corner. "We're late because your mom decided to stop at the Daveys' to see if they wanted to follow us over the moor in their car, and it's a good thing she did!"

"Why? What happened?" Mandy was about to give her gran a quick hug but remembered her straggly wig and greasy makeup and held back.

"Hi, Grandpa! What's wrong?"

"Whoa!" Tom Hope saw her for the first time. "You nearly frightened me out of my wits!" He gave Mandy an admiring grin before taking a square box covered with a cloth from Dr. Emily. Mandy's mom took a second, similar box from the Land Rover and gave it to the still-beaming Daniel. Then Gran closed the door.

"Now, no need to worry," Mandy's kindly grandfather reassured her and Ms. Temple. "But as Dorothy said, what we need is a nice, warm, quiet place for the two little unexpected visitors!"

"What *kind* of visitors?" Mandy gathered her cloak around her. The cold and stage fright were both making her shiver. Her teeth began to chatter in the icy wind.

"Hamsters!" Daniel said with a bright grin.

"Honey and Marmalade," Dr. Adam told her, coming around from the driver's side. "Can you find somewhere for us to put them while we go in and watch the show?"

Mandy stared at the two covered boxes in Daniel's and her grandpa's arms. For a few seconds, she was too surprised to answer, but now she saw what her gran had meant by "room at the inn."

Ms. Temple stepped in. "Bring them to the lab. Follow me." Quickly, she retraced her steps down the side path.

"How come?" Mandy gathered her wits and trotted alongside Daniel. Everyone was following the biology teacher in a tight file. From inside the building, sounds of the orchestra tuning up drifted out.

"We got to the Daveys' house just as Mabel decided to give birth. A real coincidence, you have to admit," Dr. Adam continued the explanation.

"I thought the babies were due this weekend." Mandy ran to hold the lab door open. Daniel and her gran, grandpa, mom, and dad followed the teacher out of the cold.

"They were, but they were late. As it turned out, the birth was complicated, so it was a good thing we were there."

"Your mom and dad saved their lives!" Daniel said. He carried the hamster cage with great care.

"Poor little Mabel had gone into labor," Gran continued. "The mother hamster needed help with her delivery."

"It was fantastic!" Daniel added.

"How many?" Mandy asked. She pictured the scene.

"Six," Tom Hope reported, putting the first cage down on the shelf next to Henry, where Ms. Temple had shown him. He took off the cover and leaned forward to check that Marmalade was OK. "Six bright pink, naked, tiny, wriggling creatures. Completely helpless."

"Fantastic!" Daniel insisted, breathless with wonder.

Mandy gasped. "How are they? How's Mabel?"

Grandpa turned to the experts.

"Doing pretty well," Dr. Emily replied cautiously. She took Honey's cage from the boy and gently put it on the shelf. As she lifted the cover, they saw a furry cream face nuzzling up to the wire mesh, peering curiously at her new surroundings. "But Mabel was exhausted after the difficult birth, and the babies are weak. Joanna and John will have to help the mother look after them for the first couple of days, and that will keep them very busy."

"So meanwhile, because they had their hands full, we offered to baby-sit these two feisty little things at Lilac Cottage." Grandpa grinned at Honey and Marmalade.

Dorothy Hope quickly finished the story. "The only trouble was, we were already late for the show. So we decided to bring the hamsters with us!"

Down the hallway in the auditorium, the orchestra was a few minutes late striking up the opening number.

"It sounds like we're going to miss the beginning after all." Dr. Adam heard the music and sighed.

"No. If you're quick, you can still make it!" Ms. Temple hurried them through the door in a jumble of jostling arms and legs. "Don't worry, the hamsters will be safe on Henry's shelf. We'll keep an eye on them for you!"

Dr. Emily closed the lab door behind her. She turned to smile at Mandy. "Good luck!" she whispered. "And by the way, dear, you look amazing. I'm sure you're going to be absolutely fine!"

Mandy stood in the wings, waiting for her first entrance. She watched the stagehands roll her house, supposedly made from the bones of shipwrecked men, into position in the middle of the stage. The house had been painted by some of the older students, and the effect was very eerie.

As the stagehands finished, a green light glowed on the witch's house, and spooky music began to play.

Mandy closed her eyes. *Please let me remember my lines!* Her throat was dry, her tongue stuck to the roof of her mouth, and her knees shook.

"You'll be OK." James stood at her shoulder, encouraging her. He'd appeared in the first scene and lived to tell the tale. "Once you get out there, it's not too bad."

She swallowed hard. The musical buildup to the witch's entrance grew louder. Down there in the front row, her parents and grandparents sat expectantly.

Thirty seconds more, and she would be under the spotlight with Susan Collins, speaking her first words.

But suddenly, out of nowhere, Daniel Winterton flashed into her mind. "Oh, no!" Mandy gasped, staring at a gap in the front row of seats. It could only mean one thing.

"What?" James stared at her as if she'd gone crazy, his glasses glinting green from a reflection of the overhead lights.

"Daniel's not in his seat!"

"So?" James turned her around to face the stage. Any second now, the cymbals would clash, and Mandy would have to make her entrance.

"He's up to something!" Mandy said. "I don't know what, but now that I think of it, I didn't see him leave the biology lab with the rest of us. He could still be in there with Henry! And Honey and Marmalade!"

"Mandy, what are you saying?" James spread his hands helplessly.

"I don't know exactly!" she hissed. The cymbals clashed. She clenched her fists and got ready to enter. "But I've got this strange feeling!"

"Stage fright," he muttered.

"No. James, I'm worried about the hamsters!"

Crash, clash, rumble! That was Mandy's cue.

"OK, I'll go and check," he promised as Mandy swooped onstage.

The green light flashed purple, and there was a mighty drumroll.

"I already know what you want!" Mandy said with a horrible cackle. "You want to get rid of your fishtail and have two stumps to walk on like human beings. It is very unwise of you!"

She heard the children in the audience gasp at her green face and long, pointed fingernails. Whirling her cloak around her, making the paper snakes squirm across the stage, Mandy forgot for the moment all about James, Daniel Winterton, and the three furry hamsters.

Seven

The Witch of the Sea told the Little Mermaid that she would grant her wish. Eerie music played as she mixed a magic potion. Then she whirled her black cloak around her with a cackle. *"Waagh-haagh-haagh-ha-ha-ha-haagh!"* The stage lights flashed green and purple, and the scene ended on a roll of drums and screech of violins.

"Phew!" Mandy was offstage, standing in the wings with Susan, amazed that she'd made it. Her legs felt like jelly.

"You were great!" Susan grinned at her, pausing before she hurried off to change her costume.

"Really?" It had all happened in a blur of overhead lights and loud music.

"Yes, really!"

The next scene was already under way. Mandy wouldn't be needed again for at least fifteen minutes, so she made her way along the ground-floor hallway, hearing the music fade into the distance as she went looking for James.

"Mandy!" He appeared at the biology lab door.

"What's wrong?" She could tell in an instant that James had bad news. He was beckoning her to hurry but keeping his voice low.

"What are all these hamster cages doing here?"

Mandy realized that she hadn't had time to fill James in on the latest events. She tried to explain as quickly as she could, then focus on her worries about Daniel. But he cut her short.

"OK, OK, I get the picture. And you were right to send me to check," he told her, pulling her in through the door and closing it after her. "Come and look!"

Across the room, the three hamster cages sat side by side on the shelf. Inside one, Mandy saw Henry trundling happily inside his wheel, spinning it fast, almost as if showing off in front of his visitors. His pink ears were laid flat against his head, his feet scrabbled at the rungs, and his little backside swayed as he ran.

Then she looked in the next cage. Marmalade, the Daveys' long-haired cinnamon-colored hamster, had his face pressed eagerly against the bars of his cage. His nose was squashed flat, and his whiskers poked through, as if he was pleading to be let out to play.

But then Mandy looked at the third cage. There was a pile of wood shavings in one corner and a plastic tube for Honey to play with in another. The food dish at the front of the cage had been upturned and seeds and nuts were scattered across the floor. But there was no silky fawn creature with bright black eyes peering out, no Honey picking at the spilled food with dainty paws . . . nothing . . . no hamster in there at all!

"Where's Honey? Where's Daniel?" Mandy spun around. Her fears seemed to be confirmed.

"Search me!" James stood by helpless as the news sank in. "He wasn't here when I arrived, and neither was what-do-you-call-her — Honey." He took off his glasses and wiped them on his shirt, giving himself time to think. "You don't suppose Daniel's stolen her, do you?"

Mandy searched the shelf, behind stacks of books and packets of hamster food. She remembered the last time Henry had vanished. "He wouldn't — would he?"

"You know how crazy he is about hamsters." James obviously thought they had to consider the possibility. "And you said you thought you'd left him in here."

Mandy sighed and gave up her search along the shelf. "He was really disappointed when Mrs. Winterton told him he couldn't have another one." Her stomach was beginning to flutter as it began to appear more likely that the unhappy little boy had done something really silly this time. "We have to talk to him!" she decided.

"How long do you have before your next entrance?" James asked, taking one last look through the bars at the empty cage.

"About twelve minutes. How about you?"

James looked at his watch. "Six."

Enough time to find Daniel and ask him if he knows anything about Honey. "Let's try the side door," Mandy suggested, darting between the workbenches to push hard at the handle. Two of her witch's fingernails came loose and fell off.

"Locked," James told her, stooping to pick them up. "I already tried it."

Ms. Temple or Mr. Browning must have made sure that the building was secure after they'd brought the cages in through the side door. "Good. At least Daniel can't have stolen Honey and dashed outside into the cold with her."

"*If!*" James insisted, trying not to jump to conclusions. "*If* he has stolen her."

"OK." After the shock of finding Honey gone, Mandy

began to calm down. She took a deep breath. "Let's think. Daniel probably stayed down here when we left the lab." She began to count points off on her fingers. "So he must have hidden somewhere here and waited until everyone had left." She was so busy thinking out loud, she didn't notice James's frown as his attention switched to Ms. Temple's storeroom. There seemed to be a noise coming from inside.

"Shh!" He raised his finger to his lips.

Mandy stopped suddenly. She strained to hear.

On the wall above the door, the clock ticked loudly. In the distance, the orchestra played and the choir sang.

"Did you hear that?" James crept softly toward the storeroom door. "Someone's crying."

She followed and saw him listen at the closed door. Yes, there was a muffled sob and a sniff.

"Daniel?" James asked, trying the handle. "Don't scare him," he warned Mandy.

"What do you mean?" she hissed. Did he think she was going to rush in and pounce?

"Your costume!" James pointed out. "You even scare *me* in that!"

"Oh, it's OK. Daniel saw me in my costume when he arrived with the hamsters," she explained.

James nodded. "Daniel? It's us, James and Mandy. Can we come in?"

There was another sob, a louder sniffle. "Honey's lost!" a tearful voice wailed. "But I didn't steal her! It's not my fault!"

"Listen, Daniel, come out so we can talk." James spoke as if they had plenty of time. He sounded calm and patient as he peered in through the frosted glass panel. "Or will you let us come in there?"

"I'll come out," Daniel answered miserably. He appeared at the door, his round face tearstained, his eyes red. As he turned the handle, the storeroom door swung open and he spotted Mandy. He gasped and took a quick step back.

"It's me!" she assured him. "Remember?" She took off her hat and wig, then shook out her blond hair. "Did you know Honey was missing?"

The little boy nodded. "But it wasn't me!"

"So you don't know where she is?" Mandy couldn't help feeling suspicious. She narrowed her eyes and stared at Daniel.

"No!" he protested. Tears came back into his eyes.

"But no one else has been in the lab, have they?" Mandy felt the seconds ticking by. Soon James would have to go back onstage. At this rate, she would have to start the search for Honey by herself.

"No," Daniel admitted, hanging his head. "But I never stole her!"

"OK, we believe you. But we don't understand what's happened." The less time they had, the more patient James seemed. He led the way across the room toward the three hamster cages.

As Daniel looked up at the empty cage, his lip began to tremble.

"Are you telling us that you didn't go anywhere near Honey's cage?" James pressed him carefully.

"I never said that. I said I never stole her, even if that's what everyone thinks!"

James raised his eyebrows and glanced at Mandy. "OK. So you did go up to her cage?"

Without waiting for Daniel's answer, Mandy seized the opening. "Did you want to play with her?"

The little boy looked down at the floor and nodded. "Just for a minute."

"So you opened the cage and took her out?"

There was a long silence. Daniel shuffled his feet and sniffed. Then he nodded.

"But you put her back?" Mandy wanted to believe him. "This was an accident, wasn't it? You didn't want Honey to escape." Inside their cages, Henry and Marmalade scuffed and scuttled.

"I only played with her," Daniel murmured.

James glanced at the clock over the door. "And what happened after you put her back in the cage?"

Daniel shrugged.

"Come on, Daniel. This is really important," Mandy urged. They needed every single clue they could get to start the search for the Daveys' missing hamster. "Show us what you did."

Sighing, Mrs. Winterton's son dragged a stool underneath the shelf and climbed onto it. "I held her carefully and lifted the door, like this."

Honey's cage door had a hinge across the top. Daniel lifted the whole front of it to show them how it worked.

Mandy nodded. "Then you put her inside?"

He nodded. "I put some chips in her food bowl. She loves chips! She was so greedy, she knocked the bowl over while I was shutting the door." He showed them how he'd done this, then climbed down from the stool.

"Wait!" James said. "Show us how you closed the latch on the door."

"Like this." Daniel reached up and clumsily twisted the metal latch with his stubby fingers. He left it without managing to secure the door firmly in place.

Mandy's eyebrows shot up, and she drew a deep breath. So this was how Honey had escaped! The clock's minute hand jerked forward. "Then where did you go?" she asked Daniel.

He frowned. "I went to Mom's locker to get Honey some more chips from my bag," he told them. "There was enough to go around; some for her, and some for Henry and Marmalade. I only left them alone for a few minutes. But when I came back, the cage was empty. Honey had gone!"

"Don't tell Mom!" Daniel had pleaded. He'd begun to sob all over again when he realized what he'd done.

James had been forced to leave Mandy and Daniel in the lab and dash back for his next scene in the show. He'd promised to come back in ten minutes to spend the intermission looking for the escaped hamster.

"We can't tell her, can we?" Mandy told the little boy, offering him the edge of her cloak to wipe away his tears. "She's out in front of the stage, conducting the orchestra, so don't worry about that just yet."

"I never meant it."

"We know that. It was an accident. But Daniel, Mr. and Mrs. Davey will be really upset, so we have to do our very best to find Honey before they hear about it, OK?"

He dried his eyes and nodded.

"Because something like this could ruin Christmas for them," she explained. "And my gran and grandpa promised to take good care of Honey, so they'll feel sad that they've let them down, and that could spoil their Christmas, too."

"I'm sorry," Daniel murmured. He stared at Mandy with his big, round, sad eyes.

She nodded back. "So I'm going to leave you here in the lab with the door closed while I go back and do the witch's scene. You have to look everywhere. Find Honey for us."

Daniel lifted his chin and jutted it out. "I'll try," he promised.

"And you know those chips you went to get? You could use one or two to tempt Honey out. If she's hiding in a closet and she smells her favorite food, she might creep out for a quick snack. That's when you could catch her and put her back in her cage. Gently. Don't hurt her." Taking her example from James, Mandy tried hard to sound calmer than she felt.

"OK." Daniel took the bag from his pocket and scattered one or two chips on the workbench below Honey's cage. Inside their own cages, Henry and Marmalade twitched the tips of their noses. Food!

Mandy took one last look around the room at the teacher's desk and blackboard, the stacks of books, the wall charts and rows of benches. "Don't open the other two cages, whatever you do," she told Daniel. "And don't open the lab door to anyone except James. It's intermission after this next scene, so James and I will be back as soon as we can."

He nodded nervously. "Don't be long."

As she turned the door handle, she could hear the music building up to her next entrance. Everyone backstage would be frantically looking for the Witch of the Sea. "I've got to go!" She only had time for one final reassurance. "Don't worry, Daniel. Honey can't have gotten very far!"

"At least I hope not," Mandy muttered to herself as she slipped from the room, jamming her wig and hat onto her head as she sped along the hall. There was no guarantee that Honey would be easy to find in this maze of strange hallways and classrooms.

As she dashed onstage under green-and-purple flashing lights, Mandy knew that the tiny honey-colored hamster could be absolutely anywhere in the school!

Eight

"Daniel, would you let us in, please?" Dr. Adam was tapping at the biology lab door.

Mandy had whooshed offstage in a cloud of dry-ice smoke, giving her best cackle yet. The curtain had come down, and it was time for the intermission.

While the audience gathered for refreshments in the home economics room, Mandy had dashed back to the lab to help Daniel find the missing hamster. But here were her mom and dad knocking at the door and peering anxiously through the pane of glass.

Dr. Emily saw Mandy flying down the hall, her cloak

wafting behind her. "Who needs a broomstick?" she joked.

"Hey, Mandy, you're terrific!" Dr. Adam glanced around but kept on tapping at the door. "This is odd. Your mom decided to come and check on the Daveys' hamsters, and we know that Daniel is in there. We saw him before he noticed us. He's jammed a stool against the door and is down on his hands and knees, obviously looking for something that he's lost."

Mandy's mom made a face, then stared carefully at Mandy. "You don't happen to know what's going on, by any chance?"

Mandy sighed. "I told him not to let anyone in," she confessed.

Just then, James came running around the corner by the lockers and coatrooms. "Sorry, I got held up." He gasped and then stopped short when he saw Dr. Emily and Dr. Adam.

"It's the hamsters, isn't it?" Dr. Emily said quietly, looking from James to Mandy and back again.

"Honey," Mandy agreed. Quickly she told them the whole story, watching a frown develop on her mom's pretty, freckled face.

Her dad scratched his beard thoughtfully. "I knew Daniel was longing for Mrs. Winterton to give in and agree to have another hamster, and I felt that perhaps he wasn't quite old enough to look after one by himself just yet. I suppose this proves the point."

"What do we do now?" James went forward to peer through the door. "I can see Honey's cage from here, and it's definitely still empty."

"Daniel must be too scared to open up." Mandy craned her neck to see. She spotted a pair of sneakers and two legs sticking out from under one of the benches. The rest of the little boy's body was hidden by a cupboard. "Daniel, it's OK!" She stooped to call through the keyhole. "It's Mandy and James. Take the stool away and open the door."

Slowly, he crept out from under the bench. His face was pale, his eyes dark and frightened as he approached the door to let them in. "Honey didn't come out of her hiding place to eat the chips," he whispered sadly.

Mandy decided not to let him see how worried she was. "Mom and Dad will help us look," she told him as, one by one, they slipped into the lab.

Dr. Emily went straight to the cage and checked it. "Maybe I'd better get in touch with the Daveys and tell them what's happened."

"Not yet." Mandy's dad considered the problem. "Wait until the end of intermission. You never know,

Honey might show up once we all start looking. If not, we can call Joanna and John and warn them then."

"But I feel so responsible," Dr. Emily said with a shake of her head. Her long red hair fell across her shoulders. "I should have dropped Mom and Dad off and driven the hamsters back to Lilac Cottage instead of leaving them here during the show."

"And missed Mandy's starring role?" Dr. Adam pointed out. He did his best to make everyone feel better. "Listen, rather than blaming anyone, let's all get busy and see if we can find the runaway."

Mandy was the last one into the lab. She glanced up and down the hall before she closed the door, hoping for Daniel's sake that his mother wouldn't come looking for him during the intermission. But she felt her heart sink into her long, pointy witch's shoes when she saw the stout figure of Mrs. Ponsonby sailing toward them.

"Quick!" Mandy tried to bundle James into the room.

"Yoo-hoo, Mandy!" A cloud of flowery perfume and a loud voice announced the arrival of the owner of Bleakfell Hall.

Too late! Mandy closed her eyes and grimaced.

"Adam, I'm so glad you're here!" Mrs. Ponsonby cried, her scarlet velvet beret perched at an angle, her cream-colored Pekingese dog peeking out from under her red cape. Somehow Pandora had escaped the care-taker's eagle eye. She pushed past Mandy and James, then launched herself into a booming explanation. "I went out to take a custard cream each to Toby and Pandora, and lo and behold, I spied the Animal Ark Land Rover!"

"Er, Mrs. Ponsonby, I'm pretty busy just now." Mandy's dad tried to usher her back toward the door.

Mandy saw Pandora reach out to nip his hand as he put it on Mrs. Ponsonby's arm. Her dad snatched it away in the nick of time.

Blissfully unaware, Mrs. Ponsonby stood her ground. "When I saw your car, I said to myself, '*Carpe diem. Seize the day!*' You could say that is the Ponsonby family motto."

"Pardon?" Dr. Adam raised his eyebrows at Mandy and nodded for her and the others to continue the search for Honey while he dealt with Mrs. Ponsonby as best he could.

"Seize the day! In other words, never miss an opportunity. Or, never put off until tomorrow what you can do today! And of course, we're approaching Christmas, and I do want poor Pandora to be completely better by then!"

"Mrs. Ponsonby, I'm afraid I don't know what you're talking about."

Mandy heard her poor dad trying to cope as she went to the windows and began to raise the blinds to look behind them for a clue to Honey's whereabouts. Meanwhile, Dr. Emily had gone with Daniel to look in the technicians' storeroom, and James was concentrating his search under the radiators and behind the teacher's desk.

"Pandora — sneezing — surely you haven't forgotten my visit to the clinic in the snow!" Mrs. Ponsonby gave a whinnying laugh. "Oh, Adam, you're teasing me. Of course you remember!"

"Er . . . of course. How could I forget?" Dr. Adam coughed and stammered. "But didn't we decide that Pandora had probably sniffed some pepper on the braised steak you'd given her as a special lunchtime treat?"

"Ah, yes!" The large woman broke in triumphantly. "But she sneezed again this morning — three times. And this time she hadn't had any steak!"

"Ah!" Dr. Adam half sighed, half groaned.

"I've been worried about her all day, and when I saw your car, I decided to strike while the iron was hot!"

Making her way along the windowsills without success, Mandy bumped into James, who was looking for Honey under a radiator. He rolled his eyes and shook his head.

"Iron?" Dr. Adam echoed faintly.

"Yes. I told Toby to be a good boy and stay in the car, and I brought Pandora inside for you to have a look at her. And I'm fortunate, because I found you right away, so you have plenty of time to examine her before the play starts again!" Mrs. Ponsonby set the Pekingese down on a workbench and hovered eagerly nearby.

"Any luck? James? Mandy?" Dr. Emily poked her head around the storeroom door to ask them how they were doing.

They shook their heads and continued searching, while Dr. Adam admitted defeat and began to examine an irritable Pandora. Mandy joined James on their hands and knees, searching every inch of baseboard around the walls to see if there was a small hole that an adventurous hamster might have slipped through. As she backed toward the door, she felt it open.

"Mandy?" Grandpa's puzzled voice interrupted Pandora's low growls. "What are you doing down there? What have you lost?"

Quick-witted Gran came in behind him. She took in the situation at a glance and went straight over to the empty hamster cage to confirm her suspicions. Immediately, she, too, began to search every corner of the room.

Grandpa was slower to catch on. "Why is this cage empty?" he queried, scratching his head. "Don't tell me one of the Daveys' hamsters has made a run for it!"

"Shh, Grandpa!" Mandy warned. If Mrs. Ponsonby heard, soon the whole world would know.

"Hamster?" Sharp-eared Mrs. Ponsonby picked up the word. "Missing? Don't tell me it's that charming little boy, Henry!"

Though Mrs. Ponsonby hadn't always liked hamsters,

she'd taken to Henry when he'd found his way into a hamper full of food she'd been preparing at a campsite the previous summer. Now she left Pandora to Dr. Adam and rushed over to the three cages.

"Oh, there you are, Henry!" She spotted the golden-brown hamster peeking out of his cage and made tweeting noises with her lips. Then she went on in a singsong voice, "You wouldn't run away again, would you, dear?"

"Yuck!" Mandy squirmed with embarrassment.

"Oh, wouldn't he?" James muttered.

Mrs. Ponsonby turned her attention to him. "James dear, don't mumble. I take it you and Mandy are looking for a different hamster? And did I hear the name Davey mentioned?" This time the bossy woman swung around to confront Mandy's grandpa. "Isn't that the couple who've moved into the house next door to the post office?"

Soon she'd pieced the story together and organized a search party to look farther afield. "Tom, see if you can delay the start of the second act until the hamster has been found," she ordered.

"We can't do that!" Grandpa objected.

Mrs. Ponsonby waved her hand impatiently. "Of course we can. This could be a matter of life and death for the poor creature!"

"Please don't tell my mom!" Overhearing the latest

order, Daniel emerged from the storeroom. His sudden appearance made Pandora jump, and the chubby little dog started to yap, while Dr. Adam tried to stop her from jumping off the high bench.

"Don't tell your mom what?" A new voice could be heard from the hall. It was Mrs. Winterton herself. She came into the lab, dressed in an attractive dark blue sleeveless evening dress. "Daniel, what have you been up to?"

Pandora's yapping bark had brought Mr. Browning striding down the hallway. "Is that a dog in the building?" he demanded irritably.

"I can't find a thing wrong with Pandora," Dr. Adam tried to tell Mrs. Ponsonby, hanging onto the squirming, yapping dog above all the noise.

Mrs. Ponsonby bossed and tutted, and Daniel began to cry, while Mrs. Winterton stood silently amid the chaos. Mandy and James got slowly to their feet and brushed themselves off, dreading what would happen next.

"Things can't get any worse," James muttered, gazing at Honey's empty cage.

"Want to bet?" Mandy nudged him to make him look toward the door.

And there stood Joanna Davey, half hidden by the caretaker's broad figure. There was no mistaking her bright orange fleece jacket and her neat, shiny dark hair. She looked as if she'd just come in from the cold. Her face was fresh and rosy, her jacket zipped up to the chin.

"Hi, Emily!" she said, smiling at the confusion, thinking that noisy Pandora and Mrs. Ponsonby had caused it all. She stepped past Mr. Browning and squeezed into the lab.

Mandy stared, then backed away. For one crazy moment, she thought that if she stood in front of Honey's empty cage, she would be able to keep the hamster's disappearance a secret from her owner.

Joanna unzipped her jacket. "I came to see the second half of the play," she told them briskly. "John said he didn't mind staying at home to baby-sit Mabel's new litter. We thought it was a shame to waste both the tickets we'd bought. . . ." Her voice slowed to a halt as she looked from Emily to Adam Hope to Mandy's startled grandparents, then to Mrs. Ponsonby and Pandora.

"Ahem!" James joined Mandy in front of the shelf. He coughed and shuffled noisily.

"Never mind 'ahem!'" Mrs. Ponsonby broke the awkward silence. She bustled forward to take Joanna's hand. "I'm Amelia Ponsonby from Bleakfell Hall. You've probably heard my name in the village."

The newcomer looked blankly at her.

"The fact is, my dear, we have some bad news. Come and sit on this stool and compose yourself. Are you ready?"

Mandy watched the clouds gather on Joanna Davey's clear, bright face.

"I'm afraid that your little hamster Honey got out of her cage and ran away! But don't worry, we'll send out search parties throughout the school," Mrs. Ponsonby assured her. "We'll comb the building from top to bottom. We'll send people out into the grounds to look. With Amelia Ponsonby in charge, we won't leave a stone unturned!"

Nine

"No! Definitely no!" Mandy's gran stood up to Mrs. Ponsonby. "We can't cancel everything just to find one missing hamster!"

A bell had sounded to signal the end of the intermission. The audience was filing back into the auditorium. In the biology lab, the debate over Honey was fierce.

"It may be just one insignificant small creature to you, Dorothy Hope," Mrs. Ponsonby challenged, "but to poor Joanna, this hamster is a beloved member of her family!"

James grimaced at Mandy. Even he thought this was going a bit too far.

"I agree with Dorothy," Mandy's grandpa interrupted. "The show must go on!"

"Think of all the effort that's gone into this show," Dr. Adam reminded everyone. He gave Mandy an apologetic glance. "Sorry, dear, I'm on your gran's side. Mrs. Winterton has put in weeks of rehearsal. All the kids in the show have given up their free time, and there are hundreds of people in the audience, all looking forward to the second half."

Mandy bit her lip and nodded. *But what about Honey?* She made rapid calculations about how she and James might be able to continue the search, even if the show did go on.

Meanwhile, the red pom-pom on Mrs. Ponsonby's velvet beret was trembling with indignation. She still seemed determined to call the show to a halt. "I'm surprised at you, Adam! As a vet, I would have thought your first priority would be to help any animal in trouble!"

"Stop!" At last Joanna Davey spoke out. She stood up and went toward Mrs. Ponsonby. "Thank you," she said quietly. "Of course I'm upset about Honey, but really, there's no question of stopping the show to look for her."

"My dear!" Mrs. Ponsonby was about to dismiss her point of view. "I know you're trying to be brave, but —"

"It's OK, we can do both," Mandy cut in. Time was getting short. A second bell had rung to call the audience to their seats. "We can look for Honey *and* continue with the show!"

Mrs. Ponsonby glared at her, then suddenly changed her mind. "Exactly! This is what I've been saying all along," she blustered. "It's a question of organization. Joanna, Emily, Adam — you and I will continue to lead the search operation from here in the biology lab. Mrs. Winterton dear, you must go back to your orchestra. And Mandy and James, it's time for you to run along and take your places backstage!"

Mandy frowned. But there was no time to argue. For the time being, they must leave it to the grown-ups.

A final bell announced the end of the intermission and the start of the second half of the show.

"What about Daniel?" James asked as he and Mandy dashed along the hallway. Mrs. Ponsonby had overlooked the very person who was responsible for the hamster's disappearance.

Mandy shrugged and headed for her stage-left entrance. She pulled the wide brim of her witch's hat firmly down and prepared to go onstage. "I don't know. I just wish there was a magic spell to get rid of Mrs. Ponsonby!"

James grinned. "You don't trust her to find Honey?"

"No way!" Mandy pictured the chaos that Amelia Ponsonby and Pandora might cause. "If I was a hamster in hiding and I saw that red pom-pom and ball of yapping cream-colored fur heading toward me, I'd run a mile!"

Mandy's part in the second half of the show was smaller than in the first. She had a scene with the Little Mermaid's seven sisters where they pleaded with her to save the mermaid and bring her back to the sea. There was more mixing of magic potions, more hissing and cackling before she sent the sisters off on their mission of mercy. After that, she was free until the finale.

Mandy went through her speeches without a flicker of stage fright. Confidently, she whirled her cloak and clawed at the sisters with her long fingernails. She threw foam-rubber toads into her boiling cauldron with gay abandon. One last screech, and she was gone.

Offstage almost before she knew it, she had at least half an hour before she was needed again.

Now! she thought to herself. *Now for the serious business of finding Honey.*

First, she had to find out how far the grown-ups had gotten, but she hoped to do this without crossing Mrs. Ponsonby's path. Since she was probably still in the lab organizing the others, Mandy decided to try the home economics room and other nooks and crannies along the ground-floor hallway.

She found her grandparents among the cookbooks and cake tins. "Any luck?"

They shook their heads.

"If Amelia Ponsonby calls me 'Dorothy dear' once more, I'll . . . I'll . . . !"

"Explode," Mandy's grandpa concluded. He lifted the lid of a round tin and looked inside. "Sorry we missed your second half," he told Mandy.

"That's OK. Have you seen James lately?" She knew that he, too, had a gap before he was needed onstage for his final scene.

Her grandpa nodded. "Heading thataway with little Daniel." He pointed down the empty corridor toward the lockers.

Mandy scooted off. She went into the cloakroom and found both James and Daniel Winterton scouring the area.

Hearing her footsteps, James glanced around. "We think Honey managed to slip out of the lab," he told her.

"How do you know?" Quickly, Mandy began to test the locker doors and peer inside those that opened.

"We don't know for sure. But it turns out that Daniel's bag of chips was crushed and had a hole in it. He left a little trail of crumbs out in the hall. Our hunch is that Honey might have followed it." James went on looking.

Once more, Mandy had the panicky thought that the school was big and the hamster very small. She jerked open more locker doors. Moving sideways, she heard a crunch underfoot. She looked down and saw that she'd stepped on a chip. As she stooped to brush it off the sole of her black pointed shoe, she glanced under the row of lockers.

"Oh!" She gasped, then froze. "H-H-Honey!"

A tiny, furry face stared back from the shallow gap. White whiskers twitched, black eyes glinted.

Behind her, James and Daniel crept to look. Three pairs of human eyes stared at one beady black pair of hamster eyes. Three huge faces pressed against the polished floor, gazing at one sweet, honey-colored hamster.

"Here, Honey!" Mandy breathed.

The hamster retreated farther under the lockers.

"Try reaching her!" James muttered.

Gingerly, Mandy slid her fingers into the gap.

Honey shuffled backward against the wall.

"Careful!" James warned.

Mandy stretched her arm and hand until her fingertips touched something soft and furry. "Almost!"

Daniel said nothing. He held his breath and peered into the space.

Mandy's fingers closed around a warm, small body. So, so near! "Ouch!"

The hamster had bitten her. She climbed over Mandy's hand and out of reach.

"She's getting away again!" Daniel cried.

"Which way?" Mandy couldn't see what was happening.

"This way!" James crawled toward the boys' coatroom door. "No, that way!" He changed direction and headed toward the girls' room.

Getting to her feet, Mandy tripped on her cape and stumbled over Daniel. James had crawled as far as the doorway into the girls' coatroom and was pointing through a narrow gap.

"She ran in there!" he hissed.

Mandy opened the door and followed the hamster, shivering as icy air from an open window hit her. The tiled floor was freezing cold. There were a dozen cubicles with gaps under the doors, a radiator, and a wastepaper basket at the far end, and above that the window to the outside world.

It wasn't hard for Mandy to spot where Honey was headed. The hamster's cream-colored fur showed up plainly against the dark tiles as she scuttled down the aisle between the cubicles and leaped for the wastepaper basket, clinging to its wire sides and hauling herself up.

For a few vital seconds, Mandy hesitated. Should she try to grab for Honey and risk knocking her off the basket?

"Get her, Mandy!" James peered in through the door. "Quick, before she reaches the windowsill!"

She did as he said, but not soon enough.

Honey had scrambled up from the basket to the sill,

her back legs dangling dangerously until she hauled herself to safety. Her feet slid across the polished tiled surface, sending her skidding toward the edge again. Then she regained her footing and headed for the open window.

"Now!" James urged. Honey's front legs were already reaching for the stone sill outside the window. Her rear end was tipping upward and hopping over the ledge.

Mandy made a rapid lunge, and the hamster gave a quick flick of her squat hind legs. She was gone — out of sight through the gap in the window, into the dark, cold night.

"Now she'll die!" Daniel's voice was hollow with shock. "She'll freeze to death!"

"Not if we can help it!" James was already heading for the nearest door to the school grounds, followed by Mandy and Daniel. But even he wasn't prepared for what greeted them when they stepped outside.

"It's snowing!" Mandy gasped.

Huge snowflakes drifted from the black sky and settled on the path. There was a thin covering on the parked cars, the strips of grass, and the row of holly trees beyond. Yet the sky had been clear when they'd driven here in the early evening, and no snow had been forecast.

"At least it means we'll be able to see footprints!" James said. He picked out the window through which Honey had escaped and stopped below it.

Mandy stepped out into the snow with a shiver. "Come on, we can't let Honey down now!" she urged Daniel. "Think of what Norvik would have done! He would have braved the freezing cold and saved everyone in the castle!"

The little boy nodded. His head went up and his shoulders back as he followed Mandy out into the cold.

"Can you see anything?" She took Daniel with her down the sloping path to join James. There were bushes that the hamster could have jumped into at the foot of the window.

James put out his arms to hold the others back. "Don't step anywhere near where she landed," he warned. "We need to be able to see the footprints."

"But the snow's covering them up fast." Mandy crouched down to find a clue. Soft white flakes landed swiftly and silently. In the dim glow the cloakroom light cast across the shadowy ground, it was difficult to see anything as small as the prints left by a tiny hamster.

"Over here!" Daniel called. He'd stayed on the path, where the light from the lamp in the parking lot was brighter and was now pointing to scuff marks in the snow.

Mandy and James hurried over. The marks had definitely been made by a tiny animal with sharp claws.

"They're heading this way!" Mandy took up the trail,
pointing to a gap between two parked cars. "No, I've
lost them!" She sighed. The tracks stopped beside one
of the cars.

"No, look!" Daniel found them again. He picked up
the trail across the car's snow-covered hood — tiny
footprints leading toward an overhanging holly tree.
The tracks ended at the very edge of the hood.

"Is it my imagination, or is the bottom branch on that
tree moving?" James said quietly.

Mandy followed the direction of his pointing finger.
Sure enough, the slim branch of dark green, prickly
leaves swayed and dipped in the lamplight. She had a
glimpse of bright red berries as the twig moved again.
There was a flurry of falling snow and a fleeting glance
of a small, pale animal scuttling for cover among the
leaves.

Lifting her face, Mandy stared up at the tall, dark tree.
"Honey's hiding in the holly!" she whispered to James
and Daniel, feeling the freezing touch of the soft falling
snow.

Ten

"Go and get my mom and dad!" Mandy kept her eyes fixed on the small, shivering shape of Honey the hamster. "Go, Daniel! Bring them here as quick as you can!"

As the little boy stopped hesitating and ran off, she confided her main fear to James. "Hamsters hate the cold. They belong in warm deserts, not countries where it snows. Daniel was right. Honey will die if she stays out here for much longer!"

James stared at the prickly branches of the holly tree as the hamster quickly climbed out of reach. "I could try to bring her down," he suggested.

"She wouldn't let you get near her." Judging by recent

experience, the little runaway was determined not to be caught. "You'd only scare her, and she'd probably give us the slip. Then we'd be back where we started."

"So we wait for your mom and dad?" James craned his neck and gazed anxiously into the tangle of ever-green leaves at the spot where Honey now squatted in the angle formed between a branch and the main trunk of the tree. "Will they know what to do?"

"I hope so." Mandy crept closer to the tree, relieved to see that at least the holly leaves sheltered Honey from the snow. But the hamster sat hunched and un-happy, her dark eyes blinking down at Mandy and her eyelids slowly beginning to close. "James, she seems to be going to sleep up there!"

"Oh, no! We can't let her!" He pushed forward to join Mandy. "You know what that would mean?"

Honey huddled against the trunk, eyelids drooping.

"What?" Mandy kept her voice low, predicting the an-swer James would give.

"That she's drifting into unconsciousness because of the cold — hypothermia!" he whispered back.

Mandy knew from her parents that this was where the body temperature dropped so low that an animal or person could no longer stay awake. Once they lost con-sciousness, it was usually the end. "You're right. We can't let her fall asleep!" she decided. Now there was no time to wait for her mom and dad. Instead, she began to hitch up her long black skirt, ready to climb.

"You'll get scratched to pieces!" James stepped in front and took her place.

"But I've got my cape!" Mandy insisted. "And we have to wrap Honey in something warm as soon as we reach her!" She set her foot on the bottom branch, feeling more snow slide from the leaves as she put her weight on it and hauled herself off the ground.

Pushing up between the branches, Mandy felt a hundred sharp pinpricks on her arms and legs. Still out of reach on her overhead perch, Honey scarcely moved. Her eyes blinked once, twice, three times. Then they stayed shut.

"Too late!" James saw the hamster sway unsteadily on the branch.

Mandy chose another foothold and climbed again. This time, she could almost reach out with her fingertips and touch Honey. But not quite.

"Mandy, she's unconscious!" James had given up hope. "Any second now, she's going to fall!"

The leaves scratched at her skin and pulled at her clothes, but Mandy climbed to the next branch. And now she could reach. With trembling hands, she stretched across. Her fingers closed around the hamster's shivering body, and she plucked her from the tree.

Honey's eyes flickered open as Mandy balanced on her branch and cradled her. Swiftly, Mandy eased the cloak from her shoulders to wrap it around the trembling creature.

"Is she still alive?" James called anxiously from below.

"Yes! But barely!" Mandy knew hypothermia made a patient sleepy and confused. You had to keep them warm, try to make them stay awake. Gently, still balancing precariously, she began to rub the hamster's fur with her cloak.

"Here comes Daniel with your mom and dad!" James called. He turned and called them. "Dr. Emily, Dr. Adam, over here!"

Mandy heard a burst of loud music from inside the school as doors opened and help arrived. "James, I'm stuck!" she hissed. With both hands cradling Honey in the bulky black cape, how on earth was she going to climb back down to the ground?

"You two go and help Mandy. I'll get a blanket and stuff from the Land Rover." Dr. Emily spoke quickly to Mandy's dad and Daniel.

"Bring the spare infrared lamp that we brought with us from the Daveys' house!" Dr. Adam called after her. He ran to James, closely followed by Daniel. They all stared up at Mandy and Honey.

"How is she?" Daniel called in his high, tense voice.

"Still conscious!" Mandy rubbed and massaged the tiny body. Honey's black eyes blinked, her round ears and long whiskers twitched. Mandy was so busy concentrating on keeping the hamster alive that she forgot where she was.

"Whoa, Mandy. Watch out!" her dad called up as she swayed and almost fell.

Mandy wobbled and jolted back against the trunk. She glanced dizzily at the ground.

"Sit down!" Dr. Adam instructed. "When your mom brings a blanket, I'll send James up onto the branch below you, then Daniel, then me. We'll form a human chain for you to pass the hamster from one to the other. Mandy, did you hear that?"

"Yes." She held her breath, petting and rubbing the weak creature cradled in her hands.

"OK. We're ready!" Her dad took the blanket from Dr. Emily, handed it to James, and sent the two boys up the tree.

The whole tree shook with their weight. Mandy held Honey tightly.

"OK, Mandy!" James climbed until he was within reach. He passed the thick red blanket to her. "Wrap Honey up, and hand her to me!"

Carefully, without letting the cold air get to her again,

Mandy followed instructions. Soon she had the hamster safely snuggled inside the blanket.

"Easy does it!" Dr. Adam instructed from below. "That's right; James has her. Now, Daniel, you get ready."

Slowly, smoothly, the hamster was handed from Mandy to James, from James to Daniel, and finally from Daniel to Dr. Adam, standing with two feet firmly planted on the snowy ground.

"Now, come down as quickly as you can," Dr. Emily told them as Mandy's dad took the lamp, turned, and headed indoors with the tiny patient.

Mandy looked down, her head spinning. "How did I get up here in the first place?" She couldn't remember which branches she'd used or how she'd climbed up through the spiky leaves.

The headlights of a car driving in through the gates helped her. The lights shone on the holly tree as Daniel, then James, then Mandy slowly made their way to safety. After the car stopped, the headlights stayed on, catching the children in a bright spotlight as the car door opened and closed, and a tall figure came hurrying across the snowy parking lot.

"Daniel?" The man sounded puzzled as he drew near. "Is that you?"

He stopped short of Mandy's snow-covered, bedraggled group, the collar of his padded jacket turned up, half hiding his face.

Mandy saw Daniel's eyes widen and his mouth fall open. He gasped and turned to the stranger. Then he was running away from the holly tree, up the path in the direct line of the headlights, kicking up loose snow as he sprinted across the parking lot.

The man spread his arms wide to catch him.

"Dad!" Daniel sprang at him and was lifted off his feet and swung around. "You're back!"

Mr. Winterton laughed and landed him safely on the ground. "I started for home early as a surprise, to see Mom's show. Then I got stuck in traffic on the expressway. But here I am, and not too late, I hope!" He hugged his son, then held his hand tight.

Dr. Emily grinned at James and Mandy, urging them up the slope. "Merry Christmas!" she said to Daniel's father. "You're just in time for the finale!"

Eleven

"Go and take your bow!" Dr. Emily insisted.

The last song had been sung, the final curtain had come down, and the audience was beginning to clap as actors, dancers, and musicians came back onstage.

"But Mom, we need to find out how Honey is!" All Mandy wanted to do was to dash down the hall to the biology lab to see the patient. But Dr. Emily was firm. "Leave that to us. Don't let Mrs. Winterton down. Go on."

So Mandy unhitched her snow-covered skirt and flung her cloak back around her shoulders. She rammed her bent hat down on her head and stomped off down the hallway. "I will if you will," she muttered to James.

He nodded, and they split off from Daniel and Mr. Winterton to head for the stage, just in time for James to take his bow with the rest of the prince's courtiers.

As she stood in the dark wings, waiting for her turn, Mandy felt the snow on her hat and wig begin to melt. Water dribbled down her forehead and dripped off the end of her nose. Her feet squelched in her pointed shoes.

"Go on, Mandy!" Susan Collins urged as the witch music played.

Squelch, squelch, squelch! Mandy dripped and dribbled onto the stage under the hot overhead lights. When she bent her head to take her bow, the last chunks of melting snow slid from the brim and landed in a wet puddle at her feet.

The audience cheered. A sea of hands clapped. At the back of the hall, she caught sight of her grandparents standing by the door, smiling proudly.

"Easy!" Mandy whispered to Susan, who came on last of all to take her bow. "There's nothing to this acting stuff!"

Susan grinned. "Says you!" She bowed and lapped up the applause. In the front row, her mother and father stood and cheered.

Then the lights dimmed, and the curtain came down for the very last time.

"That's the best play the school has ever put on!"

Mandy overheard the head teacher, Mr. Wakeham, congratulating Mrs. Winterton as she and James dashed offstage. "Really excellent. A credit to us all!"

"I wonder if Mrs. Winterton knows that Mr. Winterton is here?" James ran along the ground-floor hallway to keep up with Mandy.

Mandy had gathered her long, damp skirt around her knees and was sprinting to get the latest news about Honey. Her arms and legs were aching from dozens of tiny scratches made by the holly leaves, and her shoes still squelched with every step.

"Hey!" Mr. Browning saw from a distance the mess she was making of his nice polished floor.

They ignored him and sped toward the lab.

Mandy burst through the door first. Her mom and dad, Joanna Davey, Daniel, and Mr. Winterton, and, last but not least, Mrs. Ponsonby and Pandora were crowded around the three hamster cages on the shelf. Everyone was looking anxiously at the cage with the special lamp clipped to the wire-mesh front, carefully angled to direct heat inside.

Mandy and James came to a halt. Dr. Adam was still at work, carefully watching the effect of the infrared lamp on his patient. It seemed that everyone was holding their breath.

Slowly, they went to join the group. They heard the

squeak of Henry's exercise wheel breaking the silence and saw that the school hamster hadn't been put off his stride by the large group of spectators around his cage. He trod steadily, making his nightly run.

And Mandy noticed that Marmalade, too, had ignored the crisis. The bright cinnamon hamster was sitting on his haunches at the front of his cage, quietly licking his paws and using them to groom his fat cheeks and round, hairy ears. When he saw Mandy and James join the group of anxious onlookers, he cocked his head to one side, as if to ask, "Why all the fuss?"

"Well?" Joanna Davey said at last. She moved toward Dr. Adam and let James and Mandy have their first glimpse of Honey's cage.

The patient sat hunched up, a little round ball of silky cream-colored fur, her head pulled in toward her chest, her black eyes closed.

"Her pulse and temperature are back to normal," Mandy's dad reported. "The infrared seems to have done the trick. This hamster is going to be just fine!"

"Of course, if it hadn't been for Pandora, the whole story would have had an unhappy ending!" Mrs. Ponsonby announced to anyone who would listen.

Joanna Davey had thanked Adam and Emily Hope

and was making her way toward Mandy and James, her face all smiles.

"How's that?" Mandy's grandpa asked. He and Gran had come straight from the auditorium, down the crowded hallway, and back to the lab. "What did Pandora do — pick up the hamster's scent?"

The mistress of Bleakfell Hall waved him away impatiently. "It stands to reason. If poor Pandora hadn't been feeling unwell, I would never have brought her in here to see Adam. And if I hadn't been here to organize the search party — well, goodness knows what would have happened!"

Dr. Emily caught Mandy's eye and grinned. Her dad winked at her.

"Of course, Mandy, James, and Daniel did play their small part!" Mrs. Ponsonby conceded. She tucked Pandora more firmly under her plump arm.

"Well, thank you, everyone!" Honey's relieved owner smiled again. She turned especially to Daniel, who was still holding his father's hand.

The little boy blushed and dropped his gaze to stare at his sneakers. Perhaps he'd looked over Joanna's shoulder and seen his mother come into the room.

Mrs. Winterton looked flushed and tired. For a moment after she'd closed the door, she sank against it and closed her eyes. The evening had obviously been a big strain.

Everyone fell silent and turned to watch her open her eyes. She saw Mandy and James in their bedraggled costumes and the knot of grown-ups by the hamsters' cages. Then she saw Daniel holding tightly on to the hand of a tall, fair-haired figure. "Mark!"

Mr. Winterton grinned and held onto Daniel. Together they went across the room. "Merry Christmas, Karen!" he murmured, kissing her cheek.

"And well done, Mrs. Winterton!" Dorothy Hope chimed in. She began to applaud the music teacher for the superb show that she'd just put on.

"Yes, great!" Mandy's grandpa agreed. "Wonderful music!"

Mark Winterton put his arm around his wife's waist. Soon everyone in the room had joined in the applause.

"What happened to Honey?" Mrs. Winterton blushed, suddenly remembering the missing hamster.

"Ta-da!" Mandy stepped forward to show her that the runaway was safely back. She grinned at Daniel. "She had an adventure in a holly tree, but Daniel helped save her."

"Ahem!" Mrs. Ponsonby made a loud, throat-clearing noise.

"And Pandora," Mandy added, with a quick, secret

smile in James's direction. "Without Pandora, none of this would have worked out right!"

"Let's get this straight. This is *not* a Christmas present!" Mark and Karen Winterton had driven over to Animal Ark with Daniel. It was a week and a half after Christmas. The cards were still hanging from the beams in the Animal Ark kitchen; the Christmas tree still glistened in the corner of the living room.

"We don't believe in buying animals as Christmas presents," Mrs. Winterton explained. She was dressed in a bright blue jacket with a red plaid scarf tied around her neck, looking relaxed and happy now that the strain of producing the school play was over.

"Good." Dr. Adam nodded. "So, Daniel, this is an *un*-Christmas present!"

The little boy stood in the kitchen doorway, his dark eyes shining. "Can Mandy and James come and help me choose?"

"Try and stop us!" James jumped up from his seat. He and Mandy had been working at the clinic that morning, helping Jean to keep things running smoothly in reception. They'd just come over to the house for lunch.

"Is that OK?" Mandy asked her mom.

"Just let me get this straight." Dr. Emily took off her white coat and hung it on a hook behind the door. She eased her long hair out of its ponytail, then turned to Karen Winterton. "You've changed your mind. You're saying that Daniel can keep a pet hamster after all?"

The teacher put an arm around her son's shoulder. "Daniel has been showing us how responsible he can be," she told them. "Every day this vacation, he has visited Lilac Cottage to help clean out Honey's and Marmalade's cages. And Mark's convinced me that Daniel deserves another chance."

"And I only have to work away from home for another six weeks," Mr. Winterton continued. "After that, I'll be back for good. I can help Daniel look after his hamster."

"He'll be able to bring the baby home in about two weeks. It'll be company for him while his dad's away again," Mrs. Winterton explained.

Mandy had watched the glow on the little boy's face as he gazed from his mom to his dad and back again. Now she grabbed her jacket. "Where are you going to get your un-Christmas present from?" She imagined driving over to Walton with the Wintertons to visit the pet shop there.

"Here, in Welford," Mark Winterton said. "Daniel wanted you and James to help him choose."

"Where in Welford?" James, too, was curious as he,

Mandy, and the Wintertons said good-bye to Dr. Adam and Dr. Emily and got into the car.

Mandy waved to her mom and dad as they pulled out into the road under the wooden Animal Ark sign. It was a clear, bright day. Almost-melted snow lay banked against the walls and in the hollows of the fields.

"At Joanna Davey's house." Mrs. Winterton put the final piece into place. "You know that one of her hamsters had babies recently?"

Mandy laughed and said yes, she did. Mabel's six youngsters had all survived their difficult birth. The Daveys had taken good care of them. Meanwhile, Tom and Dorothy Hope had given the Daveys their promised breathing space and taken Honey and Marmalade home to Lilac Cottage on the night of the school play, as planned. Now the babies were all doing well, and Honey and Marmalade were back with the Daveys.

"Great! We get to see Honey again!" James grinned.

Welford Village was in sight. They passed the Fox and Goose, the church, and the post office.

"Hello, everyone!" Joanna Davey was waiting on her front doorstep to greet them. She showed them into the house and took them into the living room, where she now kept all three pet hamsters. "All healthy and fit!" she reported, waving first toward Marmalade's and

Honey's cages, then toward the large nursery cage where Mabel was looking after her young ones.

Mandy took a quick look at Marmalade, then Honey. Both hamsters hopped briskly to the front of their cages and twitched their noses.

"It's as if she never had an adventure in a holly tree!" James murmured. The cream-colored hamster's cheek pouches were stuffed with food; her dark eyes were bright and shiny.

Daniel had gone over to look at Mabel and her babies. "Oh!" He gasped.

So Mandy and James went to look, too.

There, in the nest of soft blue rags and wood shavings, rested the white hamster and her two-week-old litter. She was lying on her side, letting them feed. They snuggled against her, six babies with a fine covering of silky hair, tiny round ears laid flat against their heads.

Daniel peered in and sighed.

"Choose one!" his dad instructed.

"Which?" Daniel glanced over his shoulder to ask James and Mandy.

"You decide!" they insisted.

He looked up and down the row of tightly snuggled youngsters. He chose one, then another, changing his mind until he'd gone along the whole row and was about to start again.

In the background, Joanna smiled at Mr. and Mrs. Winterton.

"That one. No, that one!" Daniel continued.

Then one baby made up Daniel's mind for him. It was a pale fawn-colored hamster. As it finished feeding, it broke away from the group and bravely approached the front of the cage, clutching at the bars with its tiny pink paws. It stared boldly at Daniel with its ruby-red eyes.

"This one!" Daniel breathed.

"And what will you name it?" His dad crouched down beside him to look.

Daniel smiled happily. "Norvik the Second," he said without a second's hesitation. "And Dad, you know what? This is the best *un*-Christmas present ever!"

Look for *Animal Ark* ®:
TERRIER IN THE TINSEL

As Mandy walked toward the Fox and Goose intersection, she saw James already waiting there. He had a duffel bag slung over one shoulder.

"Hurry up!" he shouted, waving frantically. "There's a bus coming."

Mandy sped up and arrived, out of breath, just as the bus pulled up. "We're going to be really early for meeting Gran and Grandpa," she said.

"Not if we stop by the pet shop," James said promptly, getting onto the bus.

"Why would we want to do that?" Mandy threw him a

puzzled look as she paid her fare. "Apart from looking at all the animals."

"Which you'd just hate, of course!" James joked. "I want to buy a Christmas stocking for Blackie. They have some really good ones."

"OK!" Mandy took a seat next to James as the bus drove through Welford village.

Twenty minutes later, they were opening the pet shop door. Mandy loved the rich smell of animal food and straw that greeted them as they went inside.

"Wow!" James looked wide-eyed at the display of Christmas gifts for animals. There were edible treats for every pet from parakeets and hamsters to cats and dogs. On one rack there were also toys — balls with bells inside, catnip mice, and plastic balls that dispensed treats while they were rolled.

"And look at these squeaky dog pull-toys and new leashes!" Mandy said.

"Yeah, they're great. But there are too many choices." James fiddled with his glasses and groaned. "I can't decide what to get."

"No contest." Mandy tilted her head. "A stocking, definitely! Otherwise, how will Blackie know it's Christmas?"

James laughed and reached for the biggest doggie stocking on the shelf. "Blackie's going to love this. He won't be able to move for a week once he's eaten all these treats," he said as he went to pay.

Mandy raised her eyebrows. Blackie keeping still and not demanding a walk? Not likely!

With the stocking safely stowed in James's bag, Mandy and James walked along the road to the hospital.

"Look, there's Gran and Grandpa's van," Mandy said, pointing across the parking lot.

As they approached the main door, a small brown-and-white dog came out from behind some bushes. It stopped when it saw them and hung back warily.

Mandy froze. "Look!" she whispered. "It's that Jack Russell again."

James stopped dead, too. He frowned. "Do you think it's been here all night?"

"It must be cold and hungry if it has," Mandy said worriedly. "I'm going to see if I can make friends with it."

She moved forward very slowly, careful to avoid direct eye contact with the little dog. "Hello again. Don't be afraid," she said soothingly.

The Jack Russell gave a soft whine and licked its lips nervously. It pattered sideways on its short legs but didn't run away. The metal tag on its collar jingled as it moved. Mandy peered at the tag, but she couldn't read what it said.

"I think it wants to be friends," James said in a low voice. "But it seems very timid."

The Jack Russell dipped its head, and it took a few steps forward. It whined softly.

Mandy held her breath. "That's it. Come here," she encouraged gently.

The dog blinked at her and moved closer still. Slowly, Mandy stretched out her hand and let the dog sniff it. A moment later, she felt a wet cold nose brush against her fingers.

"Good boy!" Mandy stroked the dog's white chest.

"Well done, Mandy," James whispered behind her.

"Isn't he handsome?" The Jack Russell had half closed his eyes, and Mandy risked stroking his soft ears. She was just reaching out her fingers to take hold of his collar when the little dog darted sideways and took off across the parking lot. "Oh, no." Mandy's spirits sank. Just when she was getting somewhere!

She turned around to look at James. Over his shoulder she saw a security guard coming toward them. He must have startled the dog.

The guard wore a broad grin. "You're the first person who's gotten anywhere near that crafty little beggar!"

"Crafty?" Mandy echoed, puzzled. "Why? What's he done?"

"Swiped a bag of chips earlier, that's what!"

"Were they yours?" James asked.

The guard shook his head. "A little girl dropped them as she was getting into a car. And that terrier popped out of the bushes, grabbed the bag, and took off. He's quite a character."

"Do you know who he belongs to?" Mandy asked.

"No. But I've seen him around here before." The guard shrugged and headed back to his station at the entrance of the lot.

"That's just what the aide said, isn't it?" James commented as they went in to meet Mandy's grandparents.

"Yes," Mandy agreed, feeling even more worried. "Do you think he's a stray?"

"Could be." James looked thoughtful. "We could ask around and see if any other people have seen him."

"Good idea," Mandy said. "At least we know he's had something to eat!"

"Yeah, chips," James said. "But that's not much for a hungry dog, is it?"

"No," Mandy agreed. Maybe they should start putting food down themselves, which would make it easier to get near the timid little dog.

Take your imagination on a wild ride.

THE SECRETS -OF- DROON

Under the stairs, a magical world awaits you.

Ghostville Elementary™

Welcome to Sleepy Hollow Elementary. Everyone says the basement is haunted, but no one's ever gone downstairs to prove it. Until now. This year, Jeff and Cassidy's classroom is moving to the basement. And you thought your school was scary!

BOO!

BLACK LAGOON ADVENTURES

All the kids are afraid to perform in the Black Lagoon talent show. But they have to, because mean Mrs. Green says so. Too bad if your only talent is squirting milk from your nose!

Available wherever you buy books.

www.scholastic.com

LITTLE APPLE

SCHOLASTIC and associated logos are trademarks and/or registered trademarks of Scholastic Inc.

SCHOLASTIC

LAPLT8